KB085289

언니를 놓치다

아시아에서는 《바이링궐 에디션 한국 대표 소설》을 기획하여 한국의 우수한 문학을 주제별로 엄선해 국내외 독자들에게 소개합니다. 이 기획은 국내외 우수한 번역가들이 참여하여 원작의 품격을 최대한 살렸습니다. 문학을 통해 아시아의 정체성과 가치를 살피는 데 주력해 온 아시아는 한국인의 삶을 넓고 깊게 이해하는 데 이 기획이 기여하기를 기대합니다.

Asia Publishers presents some of the very best modern Korean literature to readers worldwide through its new Korean literature series ⟨Bilingual Edition Modern Korean Literature⟩. We are proud and happy to offer it in the most authoritative translation by renowned translators of Korean literature. We hope that this series helps to build solid bridges between citizens of the world and Koreans through a rich in-depth understanding of Korea.

바이링궐 에디션 한국 대표 소설 076

Bi-lingual Edition Modern Korean Literature 076

Losing a Sister

이경자
언니를 놓치다

Lee Kyung-ja

ASIA
PUBLISHERS

Contents

언니를 놓치다

Losing a Sister

명희는 배추 된장국에 밥을 말아 몇 술 뜨곤 수저를 놓았다. 푸짐히 담긴 미역 초무침, 구운 아지, 북어찜과 산나물엔 손도 대지 않았다. 월북한 세희 언니가 만나기를 신청했다는 소식을 들은 이후 제대로 밥을 먹은 적이 없었다. 어떤 날은 솟구치는 그리움으로, 더러는 억누르기 어려운 울화로, 그리고 서글픔에 겨워서 먹고 자는 일상을 놓친 것 같았다.

말소리와 밥 먹는 소리가 와글거리는 식당엔 그러나 명희 같은 사람들도 꽤 됐다. 밥은 밀어놓고 누룽지 숭늉 한 사발 받아서도 그마저 먹지 못하고 멍한 눈으로

Myeong-hee tumbled the rice into her cabbage and bean paste soup, had a few bites and then set the spoon back down. There were other dishes, all loaded with abundance—the salad of sea-weed with vinegar, the roasted egg-plant, the dried pollack steamed with sauce, the seasoned wild roots and herbs—and these she did not even touch. She had not been eating very well since hearing that her older sister, Se-hee, who had defected to North Korea, had applied to meet her. On some days, she was overcome with a sense of yearning, but there would sometimes be anger, which was difficult for her to suppress, and then at other

말없이 허공을 바라보는 사람, 벌써 식당 바깥으로 나가 어정거리는 사람, 숫제 호텔 방에서 나오지 않은 사람도 있었다. 다섯 명으로 한정한 방문 가족을 꽉 채워 온 경우도 있지만 명희는 혼자였다.

한 달 전이었나? 적십자에서 연락을 받았을 때, 거짓말이지 싶어서 몇 번이나 세희 언니가 맞느냐, 정말 나를 만나자고 했느냐, 나를 어떻게 알았느냐, 마구 물었었다.

전화 받기 꼭 사흘 전이었다. 명희는 꿈에 세희를 보았다. 꿈에라도 보고 싶던 언니가 이제 그 희망조차 삭아버린 뒤에 나타났다. 머리를 땋아 내린 열다섯 살의 세희는 시흥 공장의 정문 앞에서 동료들과 함께 걸어 나왔는데 명희는 그 앞에서 언니! 언니! 반가워 소리쳐 부르며 발을 굴렀다. 세희는 들은 척 않았다. 명희는 화들짝 깨어서 꿈이 부고(訃告)라는 걸 깨달았다. 같은 땅에서 55년을 오가지도 못하고 살면서도 혈육이라고 당신 죽은 걸 이렇게 알리는구나, 생각했다. 슬프지도 않고 그저 황망한데 눈물이 주르륵 흘러내렸다.

장전항을 마주한 산의 경사면을 살려 지은 호텔. 명희

times she would be filled with sorrow, and in this way she seemed to have been separated from her regular routines of eating and sleeping.

The restaurant was noisy with the sounds of dining and conversation, but there were plenty of people like Myeong-hee here, as well. One of these had pushed the rice aside to have a bowl of rice broth brought instead, but had not been able to eat even that, and had just gazed out, in silence, with eyes upon nothing, while others had already left the restaurant to wander about outside, and there were some people who would not even come out from their hotel rooms. In some cases, full advantage had been taken of the allowance, with five in attendance, but Myeong-hee herself was alone.

It had been—what, a month before? Getting a call from the Red Cross, she had suspected a trick and therefore fallen into a series of questions. "Is this for real?" she had asked. "My older sister, Se-hee?" "And she said that, that she wanted to see me?' 'Well, how did she find out?"

But before that, three days prior to that call. Myeong-hee had seen Se-hee in a dream. The older sister she had longed to see, even if only in a

는 비탈길을 느릿느릿 올라갔다. 오른쪽으로 고요한 장전항, 그 뒤로 건물과 산이 바라보였다. 안내를 맡은 청년은 장전항의 일부를 현대아산에서 임대해 사용하니 정해진 구역 너머로 가선 안 된다고 여러 가지 주의사항에 넣어 알려줬다. 명희는 갈 수 없는 곳을 바라보았다. 달리면 금방인 북한 땅. 아득하고 막막했다. 행사 기간 동안 북한을 '북측'이라 부르라 했다. 55년 동안 북한이었던 이름. 단지 사흘 동안 북측이었다가 행사가 끝나면 또 다시 북한이었다. 명희를 미치게 하는 혼란은 이것만은 아니었다.

중턱쯤의 객실 쪽에서 분홍색 한복을 곱게 차려입은 백발의 할머니가 중년의 여자와 남자의 부축을 받으며 걸어 내려오고 있었다. 아들 며느리겠지. 명희는 생각했다.

"우황청심환을 드시래두."

남자가 말했다.

"어머니. 그게 좋아요."

이번엔 여자였다. 명희는 그들 곁을 지나치며 할머니를 잠깐 쳐다보았다. 대쪽 같은 거 말고는 표정이 없었

dream, had at last appeared, now when her hope had withered away. Se-hee, fifteen years old and with her hair in braids, was coming out from the Shi-heung factory, walking through the main gate with some fellow workers, and Myeong-hee, there at the gate, was so happy to see her that her feet went pattering away, and she called out, "Older Sister! Oh, Older Sister!" But Se-hee took no notice, as though she had not even heard. Taken aback, Myeong-hee woke up, and then it occurred to her that the dream had been a notice of death. She thought about how, for fifty-five years, coming and going had been impossible between them, though they had been living in the same land. 'And yet to me, since I am kin, she has given notice of her death.' She felt no real sorrow, and only a mild agitation, but then the tears did come down.

The hotel had been built on the slope of the mountains, facing the Jang-jeon Port, and Myeong-hee now slowly made her way up that slope, on foot. There was the Jang-jeon Port, calm, off to her right, and beyond it could be seen some buildings and then the mountains. From among the warnings, the young man who was their guide had explained

다. 입도 암반처럼 굳어보였다. 명희는 할머니를 쳐다본 게 죄를 지은 기분이었다. 그새 비탈길은 분주해졌다. 객실에서 옷을 갈아입은 사람들이 서두르며 나오고 있었다. 차를 타고 오던 때완 달리 복장이 화사하거나 단정해 보였다. 그러나 뭔가 수십 년 동안 박제되었던 사람들이 되살아난, 기이한 분위기였다. 겉모습은 살아났으나 감정은 아직 풀리지 않은 상태일지 몰랐다.

명희는 지정된 버스에 올랐다. 버스 안은 고요하고 무거웠다. 뭔가 곧 터질 것 같았다. 현실을 비현실로 느끼고 비현실을 현실로 느끼게 되는 기이한 어긋남에 숨이 막힌 것 같았다. 금강산으로 떠나는 날이 다가올 때, 명희는 세희를 만나면 우선 때려주겠다고 생각했던 것도 잊었다. 언니를 정말 때려주고 싶었다.

세희와 명희 자매의 아버지는 경찰관이었다. 명희를 낳고 산후바람에 얻은 병으로 어머니는 명희 세 살 나던 해에 죽고 아버지는 이미 알고 지내던 젊은 여자와 곧장 재혼했다. 남매를 낳은 계모는 성정이 간사하고 포악했다. 아버지가 없는 데선 전실 자매를 학대했고 부녀지간을 이간질했다. 계모의 편을 드는 아버지를 증

that while the Hyundai Asan company was renting these parts of the Jang-jeon Port for its own use, no-one must cross beyond the designated sections. Myeong-hee looked out on those lands into which she could not cross. Were she to run, then there she would be, in North Korean territory. So remote, so desolate. They had been instructed to refer to North Korea during the event not as 'North Korea', but as 'the northern regions'. For fifty-five years, 'North Korea'. It had become 'the northern regions' for these three days only and then, after the event, it would turn into North Korea once again. And this was not the only source of confusion driving Myeong-hee mad.

Dressed up in a pink *han-bok*, an old lady had emerged from her room and was coming down, walking with a middle-aged woman and man, one at each side and each holding one of her arms. 'Must be her son, and her daughter-in-law,' thought Myeong-hee.

"Haven't I been telling you to take some lenitive?" said the man.

"Yes, do, Mother. That's a good idea." This time it was the woman. Myeong-hee caught a glimpse of the old woman as she passed them. Her features

오하던 사춘기의 세희가 집을 뛰쳐나갔다. 시흥의 공장에 취직을 한 뒤 문간방을 세 얻어 명희를 데려왔다. 나이로는 다섯 살 터울인 세희가 명희에겐 언제나 어머니였다. 명희는 어머니 얼굴을 기억하지 못했지만, 세희는 늘 명희가 어머니를 빼닮았다고 했다.

그해 여름, 인민군이 쳐내려오고 피난을 가느라 아수라장이 됐는데 세희는 눈에 빛을 뿜었다. 새로운 세상이 왔다는 것이었다.

"돈 없고 못 배운 사람도 차별받지 않고 여자도 차별하지 않아. 머슴과 소작농이 토지를 배급받았어. 이게 꿈이나 꿔 본 세상이냐? 이게 다 장군님의 은혜란다."

더운 여름 한 철 내내 빛이 어린 눈으로 세희는 동생에게 '새로운 세상'을 이야기했다. 세상에 가장 나쁜 것이 사람 차별인데 그게 없어지니 이제 누구라도 서럽지 않게 살 수 있다고 들떠서 춤췄다. 차별이 없어지면 모두가 동무라는 것이었다. 세희는 동무들과 어울려 밤낮으로 사업과 회의에 바빴다. 명희는 그 모든 것이 무슨 의미인지 이해하지 못했지만, 덩달아 으쓱해지긴 했다. 하지만 너무 짧아서 꿈이었나, 의심스러운 그해 여름의

bore no expression except for one of stiff, up-right propriety. Her lips were hard, like granite. And having looked at the old lady, Myeong-hee felt something like guilt, as though for some transgression. Meanwhile, there was an increase in activity on the avenue, out there on the slope. People who had gone to their rooms and changed were now coming back out in a hurry. These were rather dressed up now, in clothes that were fancy or formal, quite different from what they had been wearing before on the buses coming over. Yet there was something queer in the appearance of these people, as if they had been preserved for decades through taxidermy and had now been brought all at once back to life. They shared what might have been an only superficial semblance of vitality, real emotion not yet quickened.

Myeong-hee got on the bus to which she had been assigned. Inside, on the bus, there was a heavy stillness. It was as if some explosion might occur at any second. There was a strange discrepancy that seemed to take one's breath, as reality was felt to be fantastic, and the fantastic was felt to be real. Forgotten were her thoughts of striking Se-hee upon meeting her, which she had imagined

희망은 석 달을 다 채우지 못했다. 세희는 도망치듯 황망히 '곧 돌아온다'는 말만 남기고 본능적인 불안과 초조에 휩싸인 명희를 두고 떠났다.

그 후 명희는 1년 동안, 10년 동안, 20년 동안 '곧 돌아온다'는 말을 붙잡고 놓치지 않으려 안간힘을 썼다. 그렇게 붙잡을 것이 없었다면 쉴 새 없이 파고드는 절망과 좌절, 두려움의 유혹에 제 목숨을 내놓았을 것이다.

명희는 세희가 언제 돌아올지 모르면서도 언제나 그랬듯 문간에 쪼그린 채 앉아 있었다. 비행기가 머리 위로 지나가고 가까운 곳에서 우다당탕 쿵꽝하는 폭격 소리가 들려왔다. 명희는 손가락으로 귀를 틀어막았다. 불안해서 숨이 쉬어지지 않을 때도 많았다. 비행기는 더 자주 뜨고 밤낮으로 폭격을 했다. 명희는 며칠째 배가 아팠다. 배가 아픈 동안 세희는 집에 오지 않았다. 명희가 마른 나무를 주어다 아궁이에 지펴 해둔 밥은 솥에서 그대로 상해 갔다.

그날 밤도 하늘에 별이 가득했다. 별똥별이 하늘을 긋고 사라졌다. 몇 개가 거푸 그랬다. 명희는 문간에서 쪼그린 채 잠깐 졸았다. 명희는 돌무더기 쪽에서 들리는

while the day on which they were to leave for the Geum-gang Mountains had approached. She had wanted very much to hit her older sister.

The father of the sisters Se-hee and Myeong-hee had been a police officer. With the birth of Myeong-hee, their mother had fallen ill, and she had died in the year that Myeong-hee turned three, so their father had married again, right away and to a young woman with whom he had already been acquainted. The step-mother bore him a son and a daughter, and she herself was both conniving and violent. When their father was absent, she would abuse the sisters, who belonged to his first wife, and she created strife between the sisters and their father. Because their father would always take the step-mother's side, Se-hee hated him, and as a teenager she ran away from home. She got a job at the Shi-heung factory, rented a room and then brought Myeong-hee away, as well. Older than Myeong-hee by five years, Se-hee had always been like a mother to Myeong-hee. Myeong-hee had no memory of her mother's face, but Se-hee used to say that Myeong-hee looked just like their mother.

In the summer of that year, the North Korean

여치 울음소리에 문득 정신을 차렸다.

"명희니?"

세희였다.

"방에서 기다리지!"

대답도 못하는 명희에게 등을 돌려대며 세희가 걱정했다. 세희는 명희를 잘 업어줬다.

방에 들어갔지만 불을 켜지 못했다. 폭격기 때문이었다. 등잔불이 없어도 별빛에 사물이 비쳐보였다. 세희는 배에 두르고 온 쌀을 풀어놓았다.

"언니 없는 동안 밥 잘 먹고 잘 지냈어?"

세희가 물었다. 명희는 배가 아파 아무것도 먹지 못했다는 말을 하지 않았다.

그리고 무슨 말을 했던가. 세희는 채 반 시간이나 명희 곁에 있었을까?

"명희야. 곧 돌아올 거야. 어디 가지 말고 여기서 꼭 언니를 기다려야 해. 저 쌀이 다 떨어지기 전에 반드시 돌아올 테니…… 언니 믿지? 우리가 흡혈귀 양키 놈들을 박살내지 않고는 영원히 행복할 수 없단다. 민족이 해방되지 않으면 노예처럼 살게 된단다. 언니가 하는

army descended, but despite the turmoil caused by the need to evacuate, Se-hee's eyes shone with a bright light. She said that the new world had arrived.

"They've brought an end to discrimination against their poor, against those who are not well educated and against their women! The land has been distributed among the hands and the tenants. Has there ever been such a world, even in dreams? And all is coming to pass, by the grace of the General."

That summer, her eyes bright all through that torrid season, Se-hee would talk to her younger sister about the 'the new world'. She would get excited and even dance, because the most deplorable thing in the world was discrimination, and that would be gone, so everyone would be able to live without sorrow. Without discrimination, all people would be comrades. Se-hee was busy with her comrades day and night, occupied with these programs and with meetings. Myeong-hee could not quite understand what all of it meant, but she too felt exalted, right along with them. Had it not been a mere dream after all, though, so short as it was? The dubious hope of that summer was not sufficient to fill those entire three months. Se-hee

말 알지?"

명희는 한 번도 언니를 의심한 적이 없어서 그날도
물론 믿었다. 다시 돌아온다는 말, 저 쌀이 다 떨어지기
전에 반드시 온다는 말을. 그러나 자매가 짧은 이별을
위해 부둥켜안았을 때 둘은 서로가 몹시 떨고 있음을
느꼈다. 두렵고 두려웠던 건 열두 살의 명희만은 아니
었다. 슬픔이 공포에 짓눌려 울 수도 없었던 건 명희만
이 아니었다.

쌀이 떨어지기 전에…… 한 말이 채 못 되던 쌀자루.
가을이 깊어지고 서리가 내릴 때쯤, 명희는 쌀자루 앞
에서 불안했다. 쌀을 다 먹으면 언니가 오지 못할까, 걱
정됐다. 냄비를 들고 주먹으로 쌀을 펐다 덜었다 했지
만 첫눈이 내릴 때 마지막 쌀을 다 먹었다. 농사를 짓던
주인집이 부엌 바닥을 파고 독을 묻은 뒤에 피난 짐을
쌌다. 명희는 함께 가자는 주인집을 뿌리쳤다. 언니가
여기서 기다리라고 했다며 뒷걸음을 쳤다.

"언니가 독한 빨갱이 아니유."

명희는 고개 숙인 채 주인아주머니가 자신의 시어머
니에게 수군거리는 말을 들었다. 할머니가 며느리에게

made a quick departure, which was more like an escape, leaving nothing but her words, promising to 'return, and soon', and so Myeong-hee was abandoned, with anxiety and a sense of dread rising within her by instinct.

Afterwards, Myeong-hee strove to hold on to those words, 'return, and soon', so that for a year, for ten years, for twenty years, she would not lose them. Had there been nothing for her to hold on to, she would have let go and given her life over to the temptations of despair, defeat and fear that were always eating away at her.

Myeong-hee had been sitting by the gate in her usual way, not even knowing when Se-hee would be back. Above her head, an airplane passed, and she could hear the relentless sound of concussive bombing not far off. Myeong-hee stopped her ears with her fingers. Again and again, her distress was such that she could not even breathe. The airplanes were flying with greater frequency, and the bombing went on, day and night. Myeong-hee had been suffering for a few days with a pain in her stomach. During that time, through the days while that pain was in her stomach, Se-hee did not come home. So the rice that Myeong-hee had prepared,

뭐라고 말했다. 언니가 오기나 한대? 이런 말 같이 들렸지만 명희는 듣지 않았다고 생각했다.

쌀이 떨어지고 55년이 더 지났다.

상봉단과 지원단과 보도진을 태운 스무 대 가까운 버스는 느리디느리게 움직였다. 의자 사이에서 드물게 속삭이는 소리가 들리곤 하였다. 사람들은 누가 뭐라지 않아도 숨죽여 말하고 있었다. 더러 크게 들리는 목소리는 가난하고 헐벗은 북한을 흉보거나 얕잡는 말이었다. 우중충한 옷을 입고 개울에서 빨래하는 두어 명의 아낙네. 남한 어디에서도 볼 수 없는 풍경이긴 했다. 고성의 일성콘도에 집결한 어제 오후, 간단한 설명회가 있었다. 반세기 동안 헤어졌던 혈육과 만난다 해도 체제가 다르고 사상이 달라 말이나 풍속이 같지 않은 게 있을 것이며 그 점을 서로 존중해줘야 한다는 주의 사항이 있었다. 상대편의 자존심을 건드리는 말이나 행동을 하지 말도록 당부했다. 그러나 이런 말들이 명희에겐 들리지 않았다. 달랑 혼자인 가족도 명희뿐인데 짐이라곤 등에 맨 배낭이 전부인 사람도 명희 외엔 더 보

cooked on the furnace where she had made a fire with dried wood that she had collected, just went bad, there in the pot.

That night, the sky was again full of stars. A shooting star streaked across the sky and disappeared. Several more did the same. Crouched down near the gate, Myeong-hee was nodding off into sleep. Katydids were calling from the other side of a heap of stones, and Myeong-hee woke up.

"Hey, Myeong-hee?" It was Se-hee. She spoke with concern, asking, "Why aren't you waiting inside, in the room?" and she turned and offered Myeong-hee her back. Se-hee was always good about carrying Myeong-hee.

They entered their room, but making any light was forbidden. There were bombers. Since there was no light from any lamp, what they saw was illuminated only by the stars. Se-hee set down some rice, which she had had in a bundle, bound to her waist.

"I trust you've been eating well, despite Big Sister's absence?" Se-hee asked. Myeong-hee couldn't bring herself to tell her how she hadn't been able to eat because of the pain in her stomach.

이지 않았다. 검정 바지에 밤색 점퍼. 검정 배낭. 운동화. 모두 미국 돈으로 준비하라는 돈은 천 달러였다. 난생 처음 해본 환전이고 만져본 미국 돈이었다.

명희는 한 번도 넉넉해 본 적 없이 예순 넘게 살았지만, 그리고 북한에 홍수와 가뭄이 들어 굶어죽는 사람이 늘고 탈출하는 주민들이 있다고 해도, 자신보다 언니가 넉넉하지 않다는 상상은 할 수 없었다. 55년 동안 언니가 죽었을 거란 상상은 하지 않았지만 자신보다 못 살 거란 상상도 할 수 없었다.

우리 언니가 어떤 언닌데!

이 믿음은 명희의 의지를 벗어난 신앙이었다.

해가 바뀐 겨울, 혼자 남은 명희는 언니를 기다렸다. 눈이 하얗게 내린 마당에 온종일 발 딛을 만큼 눈을 치웠다. 언니는 오지 않고 피란민이 집을 차지했다. 문산 쪽에서 내려온 일가족이었다. 남자는 할아버지와 소년. 나머지는 할머니와 아기 젖을 먹이는 젊은 부인이었다. 그들은 얼굴에 노란 병색이 도는 명희를 보고 놀랐다. 언니를 기다린다고 말해도 그들은 믿지 않았다. 하지만 그들은 명희와 밥을 나눠먹었다. 동네 빈집을 찾아다니

And what else, then, was said between them? And was it for half of an hour that Se-hee stayed, and was there, near Myeong-hee?

"Myeong-hee. I'll be back soon. Don't go anywhere, but wait here for me. I'll be back, I will, and before this rice is gone... Do you believe me? If we don't destroy those yankees, those parasites, we will never be happy. If the nation is not emancipated, we will live as slaves. Do you understand me?"

Even on that day, since Myeong-hee never doubted her older sister's words, her faith was a matter of course. Those words, that she would be back, and she would be back before that rice was gone. But when the sisters embraced each other for that short separation, each felt how hard the other was shaking. Twelve year-old Myeong-hee was not the only one who suffered a persistent fear. And Myeong-hee was not the only one in whom there was a sorrow, smothered and prevented by that fear from coming out in sobs.

Before the rice was gone... A sack of rice that did not amount to even one *mal*. It was far into the depths of that autumn, now, around the time the frost began to settle, and Myeong-hee was growing anxious over the sack of rice before her. She

며 먹을 것과 돈 될 성싶은 것을 훔쳐오던 그들은 전선이 38선을 오르락내리락 하자 서울로 떠났고 피란길에서 주인집이 돌아왔다. 그 이듬해 휴전이 됐다. 휴전은 전쟁보다 더 무서웠다. 전쟁을 기다리는 전쟁이 시작되었다. 북진통일을 하겠다고 이승만 대통령은 부르짖었다. 전신주나 벽 마다 때려잡자 김일성이라는 구호가 붙어 있었다. 뿔이 달린 괴물이 튀어나온 이빨 사이로 피를 흘리는 모습은 끔찍했다. 언니가 말한 인민의 해방자 김 장군님과 피를 빨아먹는 뿔 달린 괴물 사이에서 정신을 잃지 않으려고 명희가 얼마나 애를 썼는지 누구도 알 수 없었다. 그건 목숨 같은 비밀이었다.

명희는 눈앞이 뿌옇게 보여 손등으로 차창의 유리를 문질렀다. 그러나 여전했다. 적십자에서 연락을 받은 뒤로 문득 문득 눈앞이 하얗게 된 적이 몇 번 있었다. 어떻게 눈앞이 그렇게 흰눈처럼 하얄 수가 있는지 의문이었다.

단체상봉 장소는 온정각 휴게소. 오후 3시부터 5시까지였다. 오후 3시가 되자면 반 시간이나 더 있어야 했다. 남측에서 온 가족이 정해진 팻말이 놓인 탁자에 앉

was afraid that if she were to eat all the rice, her older sister would never come back. With a pot in her hand she would scoop the rice and she would bate it, but when the first snows were come she had eaten the last of the rice. The owner of the house, a farmer, dug a hole in the kitchen floor, buried a pot there and prepared to depart. And although Myeong-hee was invited to go away with the owners, she declined the offer. Taking a few steps back, she said that her older sister had told her to wait there, and she moved off. Still, with her head down, she caught the words of the owner's wife, whispered to her mother-in-law.

"Just a red, though, ain't she, that older sister?"

The old lady then said something to her daughter-in-law. "Won't be coming back at all, then, will she?" That was how it sounded, but Myeong-hee decided that she had not heard.

The rice did run out, and then fifty-five years went by.

There were about twenty buses altogether, carrying the reunion group, the group of supporters and the members of the media, and they all moved along very, very slowly. Whispers could be heard,

아 기다리면 정해진 시간에 북측 가족이 들어온다고 했다. 명희의 팻말이 붙은 원탁은 오른쪽 창가 쪽이었다. 팻말을 찾다가 명희는 다시 한번 눈앞이 하얗게 되어 순식간에 헛발을 딛었다. 정신을 차리자 이내 눈앞이 캄캄해졌다. 언제부터 입술을 깨물었는지 패인 자국이 제 모습으로 쉬 돌아오지 못했다.

시간은 왕왕거리며 흐르고 있었다. 촬영 준비를 마친 사진기자단. 수첩을 꺼내 들고 무엇을 적는 기자. 여러 가지 표정으로 서 있는 지원단 사람들. 다섯 명의 가족이 한 사람을 기다리는 원탁은 풍성했다. 어느 자리에서 황급히 일어서는 사람이 있었다. 의료진이 부리나케 그쪽으로 다가갔다. 안정제가 주어졌다. 우황청심환을 먹는 사람도 있었다. 왕왕거리며 지나가는 시간 속으로 마른 눈물이 차오르고 있었다. 사람들은 무언가를 보려고 눈알이 쓰라리게 집중하면서, 정작 아무것도 보지 못할까봐 초조해했다.

아주 잠깐 동안 명희는 세희 언니의 모습을 그렸다. 그저 그 모습이 스쳐 지나갔다. 열일곱 살 언니. 숱 많은 검은 머리를 탱탱하게 땋아 내린 언니. 카랑카랑한 목

at intervals and rare, given from one seat to another. Communication was kept low, under the breath, though no-one had given any such direction. Now and then, a louder voice would be audible, with scorn and derision for North Korea, impoverished and in rags. There, two or three women in plain garments, washing clothes at a creek. This was a sight that had become hard to find, of course, anywhere in South Korea. A brief meeting had been held in the afternoon of the previous day, once they had all been assembled at the Il Seong Condominiums in Go-seong. They had been warned; after half of a decade of separation, though the members of families were indeed coming together again, there were differences in institutions and in ideology, and then perhaps differences in expression and customary manners, all of which must be respected. It was asked that they abstain from doing or saying anything that might injure the pride of anyone on the other side. None of these words were heard by Myeong-hee, though. There was only herself, Myeong-hee, alone; only Myeong-hee, who had no luggage but the bag, there on her back. Black pants, a brown jumper, a black bag and sneakers. She had been told to prepare some

소리. 팔과 다리가 튼튼하고 살집이 단단하던 언니. 눈동자는 검고 볼은 불그레했다. 도톰한 입술이 말을 하려 벌어질 때면 옥수수 같은 이빨들이 돋보였다. 새로운 세상! 차별 없는 세상! 인민이 누구나 평등한 세상! 부자도 가난한 사람도 없는 세상! 타고난 능력만큼 일하고 필요한 만큼 주어지는 세상!

명희는 세희 언니의 세상에는 아무런 관심도 없었다. 기다리지도, 부러워하지도, 살고 싶지도 않았다. 그게 어떤 세상인지 상상이 안 됐다. 하지만 언니의 모습은 그려졌다. 일흔두 살. 언니라면 아직 할머니 축에도 끼지 않을 것이었다. 도무지 늙지 않을 얼굴이니까. 순간 명희의 마음이 따뜻해졌다. 자랑스런 세희 언니. 세희 언니를 자랑하고 싶었다. 명희는 자신과 언니가 닮지 않은 것도 좋았다.

벽시계가 세 시를 가리키려 할 때였다. 활짝 열어젖혀진 출입문 쪽에서 둑이 무너진 것 같은, 그러나 소리 없는 함성 같은 것이 화악 밀려왔다. 사람들이 일제히 일어서고 플래시가 번쩍번쩍 터지고 어디선가 툭툭 터지는 울음소리가 들리기 시작했다. 명희가 가슴에 훈장을

money—one thousand dollars in cash. It was the first time she had ever exchanged currency, and it was the first time she had ever touched American money.

Myeong-hee had been alive for more than sixty years, and in her life she had never known abundance, and yet it was hard for her to imagine such lack in the life of her older sister, even though she had heard that, because of flooding and droughts, more and more North Koreans were dying of starvation or defecting. For fifty-five years, she had not believed her older sister dead, and she had never been able to imagine her older sister living worse off than she herself was.

"Such an older sister she is, my older sister!"

This faith was a virtual religion, and well beyond her own will.

The next winter, Myeong-hee had gone on waiting for her older sister, alone. Snow fell and covered the yard, and Myeong-hee would have to work all day to clear it just enough so that her steps could reach the ground. Her older sister did not come, and the house was taken instead by ref-

단 회색 양복 차림의 할아버지들이 줄지어 들어오는 걸 본 건 소리 없는 함성이 느껴진 몇 초 뒤였다. 그리고 똑같은 천으로 지은 치마저고리를 입은 할머니들을 본 것도.

곧 아버지! 언니! 오빠! 형님! 삼촌! 호칭과 이름들이 서로 뒤섞이고 엉켰다. 그리고 명희도 세희 언니를 찾았다. 한 눈에 알아볼 수 있는데 도무지 보이지 않았다. 세희 언니…… 명희는 아무리 정신이 없어도 열일곱 살 처녀를 찾지는 않았다. 얼굴에 주름도 잡혔을 것이며 머리 숱도 줄었을 거란 생각은 했다. 하지만 눈이 침침해서였을까. 자꾸만 눈앞이 하얗게 되었다가 캄캄해지길 되풀이해서일까.

원탁을 찾는 번호는 남북이 같았다.

할아버지와 할머니들은 번호를 보고 찾아갔다. 번호보다 먼저 얼굴을 알아보는 사람들도 있었다. 그러나 세희 언니…… 저리 늙기도 어려울 것 같은 할머니 한 분이 명희 쪽으로 다가오고 있었다. 늙은 얼굴에 비하면 자세는 대꼬챙이같이 꼿꼿한 할머니. 표정이 없는 할머니가 팻말 앞에 와서 잠깐 숨을 고르듯, 상대편을

ugees. These were a family who had come down from the Mun-san area. An old man and a boy, its males. As for the others, there were an old lady and a young woman who was nursing a baby. They were surprised at the sight of Myeong-hee, whose face had taken on a sick yellow tint. She told them how she was waiting for her older sister, but they would not believe this. They did share their food with Myeong-hee, though. They would go around the village, stealing from abandoned houses anything that might be eaten or somehow converted to cash, and with the battle moving back and forth over the 38th parallel, they eventually left for Seoul, and the family who owned the house returned from the road, having fled as refugees, themselves. In the following year came the cease-fire. And the cease-fire was even more frightening than the war. The war of apprehension, the expectation of war, was begun. President Syngman Rhee made bold promises of a unification that would take the North. On every utility pole and on every wall hung the slogan, 'Crush Kim Il-sung!' There would be a repulsive image of a monster, as well, with horns and blood running from between its protruding teeth. No-one could have known how Myeong-hee

확인하듯, 어쩌면 예의를 지키듯 멈칫하다가 의자에 앉았다. 서울에서라면 보기 힘든 밤껍질 같은 얼굴색. 일부러 고랑을 지어놓은 듯한 깊은 주름. 메마른 몸피. 사람이 제대로 먹기만 해도 저런 얼굴, 저런 모습이긴 어려웠다. 명희는 소란하고 어수선하고 말로는 표현할 수 없는 억압된 격정들이 상식의 더께를 깨고 솟구쳐 오르는 실내에서, 다만 홀로 고요했고 홀로 적요한 침묵에 휩싸인 채 굳어버렸다.

"명희가 왔구나."

언니는 어디 있지? 엉뚱하게도 이런 생각이 들 때였다. 명희가 왔구나. 마주 앉은 대꼬챙이 할머니가 엉뚱하게도 청춘의 목소리로 말했다. 명희가 왔구나. 하지만 명희는, 명희가 왔구나, 라는 말소리에 언니는 어디 있지? 라고 덮개를 덮었다. 그리고 또 다시 침묵이 흘렀다. 어느 탁자로는 남북의 보도진과 남북의 진행요원들이 모여들어 작은 잔치판이 벌어졌고 어디선가 억제하지 못한 흐느낌이 울려오고 어디서는 작은 웃음소리, 어디서는 묻고 대답하는 말소리 어디서는 장군님! 이라는 호칭들이 들려왔다. 명희는 언니라고 말하고 싶었

struggled against losing her mind, trying to reconcile General Kim, the liberator of the people of whom her older sister had spoken, and that horned monster that fed on blood. She kept this as her secret, as she did her life.

Myeong-hee wiped at the bus window with the back of her hand because the view there before her eyes was cloudy. But still it was the same. What was before her eyes was going white again, as it had done several times since the Red Cross had first contacted her. She wondered how it could be, that what was before her eyes could be so white, like snow.

And then the On-jeong Gak Park Station, the site of the mass re-union, to take place from three to five p.m. Half an hour remained, before three o'clock. The families who comprised the delegation from the South were instructed to sit down and wait at tables, to which signs had been attached, and at the appointed time the delegation from the North would enter. The round table with Myeong-hee's sign had been placed near a window. While Myeong-hee was looking around, trying to find this sign, her vision blurred, and she stumbled. And

다. 언니라고 불러보고 싶었다. 그러나 결코, 절대로, 언니여선 안 되는 할머니의 얼굴을 차마 마주볼 수가 없었다. 때려잡자 김일성. 북진통일. 간첩단 등등. 사상적으로 반목하는 민족끼리 서로 폄하와 증오를 쌓고 또 쌓아갈 때도 명희는 그 속에 언니를 상처받지 않도록 간직했었다. 명희에게 세희 언니는 그런 것들과는 아무 상관이 없었다. 언니가 말하던 세상. 가난하지도 않고 차별받지도 않는 세상이 있을 테니까.

언제 손을 탁자에 얹었을까. 명희는 그 위에서 흔들리는 손을 탁자 아래로 감췄다. 떨리는 건 손만이 아니었다. 몸도 덜덜 떨렸다. 몸이 차다차게 얼어든 지 오래였다.

"어……어……니이."

명희는 말하고 싶었다. 그러나 목소리는 가위 눌린 듯이 입술만 실룩거리며 소리로 새어나오지 못했다. 이때 할머니 세희가 탁자 위에 얹었던 보자기를 풀기 시작했다. 저게 뭘까. 혹시 55년의 뭉텅일까? 여러 개의 동전 크기 메달과 낡은 상장과 사진첩이 드러났다. 명희는 탁자 밑에서 열 손가락을 문질렀다. 손가락이 바서지듯이 아팠다.

then as soon as she had recovered her stability, her vision went black. She must have been biting down hard on her lips, and for some time, as they were gouged and would not recover.

Time passed, accompanied by a dull cacophony. A group of photo-journalists who had concluded their preparations for shooting. A reporter taking out a note pad and writing in it, and some members of the group of supporters standing around, wearing a variety of expressions. One of the round tables was well provided, with five members of a family waiting for a single relative. Someone got up quickly from a chair. The medical team made their way over. A sedative was administered. Some people were taking lenitive. And the body of this time that was passing with cacophony was being filled in with what would have been tears had they not been dry. People strained their eyes, trying to catch sight of anything, anxious and afraid they would see nothing.

Myeong-hee summoned an image of her older sister, Se-hee, but only for a very brief moment. And then the image was gone. Her older sister, at seventeen years old. Her older sister, with rich, black hair knotted tight. That clear voice. Her older

"……위대한 김일성 수령님과 김정일 장군님의 은혜로 나는 이렇게 잘 살았다. 이 훈장들을 봐라."

세희가 맨 처음, 명희가 왔구나, 할 때와는 전혀 다른 음색으로 그래서 성마르게 들리는 음성으로 크게 말했다. 김정일 배지를 단 지원단들이 웃는 얼굴로 원탁 사이를 느릿느릿 걸어 다니고 있었다. 원탁에서는 누구나 지금 그렇게 하고 있었다. 명희는 배가 아팠다. 미군 비행기의 공습이 밤낮을 가리지 않을 때, 세희 언니의 희망에 넘치던 얼굴에 긴장감이 서릴 때, 미제 원쑤들이라는 말을 자주 입에 올릴 때, 배가 아파 밥을 먹지 못할 때처럼 지금 명희는 배가 아팠다. 두 손으로 아랫배를 움켜잡았다. 이럴 때 세희는 자신이 위대한 김일성 수령님과 장군님의 크나큰 사랑으로 얼마나 행복하게 살았는지, 민족통일과 해방의 일꾼으로 보호받았는지…… 말하고, 말하고 또 말했다.

"언니."

이윽고 명희가 울면서 언니를 불렀다. 세희는 정작 대답하지 않았다. 마치 녹음기를 틀어놓은 것처럼 자신의 영웅적 삶과 수령님과 장군님의 사랑을 되풀이해서 말

sister, whose arms and legs had been so strong, and whose flesh had been so firm. Her eyes were dark, and her cheeks, red. And what a fine impression was made by her teeth, like kernels of corn, displayed by her full lips as they parted to speak. A New World! A world without discrimination! A world where all people were equal. A world where no-one was rich, and no-one was poor. A world where each would work according to natural ability, and each would receive according to need.

Myeong-hee had no interest in that world of her older sister Se-hee. She wasn't expecting it, and it inspired nothing like envy in her, as she had no desire to live there. She could not imagine what kind of world it could be. She could summon an image of her sister, though. Seventy-two years old. But her older sister would not be one of those old ladies. Never growing old, that face of hers. And this warmed her heart. Her older sister, Se-hee, making her proud. And about her older sister, Se-hee, she herself wanted to boast. Myeong-hee was glad that her older sister did not resemble herself.

Now the clock was showing almost three. From the entrance, wide open, there came a sudden rush, as if a dam had broken, but with a roar that

했다. 여섯 명이 앉을 수 있는 원탁은 명희와 세희에겐 참혹하도록 넓고 또한 멀었다. 화목하게 사진을 찍고 손을 맞잡고 볼을 부비는 가족들에겐 남북의 보도진들이 기다렸다는 듯이 쫓아가 되풀이 연출을 부탁했고 눈이 침침한 어머니 앞에 큰절을 올리는 아들의 모습도 찍혔다. 반세기 넘도록 외동아들을 기르며 홀로 살아온 남쪽의 아내와 재혼해서 여러 자식과 수많은 손자들을 둔 북측 남편. 그들도 좀체 말을 나누지 못했다. 연좌제에 걸려 하고 싶은 공부를 다 하지 못한 아들도 한참 울었고 할아버지가 도무지 낯선 손자는 얼얼한 표정으로 할아버지의 훈장이며 메달을 구경했다.

명희의 두 시간은 다른 사람들과 마찬가지로 먼지같이 훌훌 날아갔다. 북에서 온 사람들이 먼저 자리에서 일어섰고 그들은 저절로 자석처럼 따라붙은 남측의 가족들의 배웅을 받으며 문을 나섰다. 두 시간 후에 만찬이 있을 것이었다. 두 시간 후에 다시 만날 것이었다. 정해진 대로.

명희는 세희가 자리에서 일어서도, 무어라고 말해도, 보지 않고 듣지 않았다.

had no sound. Everyone rose in unison, flashes exploded from the cameras, and bursts of crying could be heard. Myeong-hee felt that sound and then, after a few seconds, she saw the old men, dressed in gray suits and decorated with medals upon their chests, all in a line and coming in. She saw the old ladies, too, wearing traditional dresses and tops, all made from the same cloth. Father! Older Sister! Older Brother! Uncle! Names and forms of address were thrown together and became entangled with each other.

Myeong-hee tried to find her older sister, Se-hee. She was sure she would recognize her at a glance, and yet that She-hee was not to be seen. My older sister, Se-hee... Myeong-hee was feeling faint and confused, but not so much that she would be looking for a girl of seventeen. She did assume there would be some wrinkles in her face, and her hair would have grown thin. Perhaps it was her eye-sight, having gone too dim. And what was before her eyes, going white and going black, again and again.

The numbers by which the round tables were to be found by those from the North matched the numbers by which those from the South had iden-

북측 사람들이 빠져나가자 두 시간의 흥분 그리고 그 이전의 기대와 두려움과 분노와 회한들이 모두 거짓말처럼 사라졌다. 아직 자리에서 일어서지 못하는 남측 사람들의 표정은 대부분 허탈과 좌절에 절망과 침통에 개운함까지 뒤섞여 기이함을 자아냈다. 천만 개, 이천만 개의 잿더미 위. 그 상징의 한곳에 성급히 꾸며진 가설무대는 아무렇지 않게 철거되었고 그 아무렇지 않은 것에 적응하지 못한 이산가족들은 자리에서 일어서지 못했다.

이윽고 북측 사람들이 모두 나가고 남측 사람들도 자리를 비운 뒤에도 명희는 의자에서 일어설 수가 없었다.

이건 아니야!

명희는 세차게 머리를 흔들었다. 언니가 진짜 그 세희 언니라면, 이건 아니야! 언니가 그런 모습이서도 안 돼! 잘 살았다니! 언니가 세희 언니라면 먼저 나한테 미안하다, 약속을 못 지켜서. 이런 말을 했어야지. 그리고 용케 살아남았구나. 그랬어야지. 그래야 세희 언니잖아. 보고 싶었다고. 하루도 잊은 날이 없었다고. 그래야 세희 언니가 맞잖아. 이건 아니야. 정말 아니야. 용서할 수

tified their own places.

Looking at numbers, the old men and the old ladies found their places. Some people discovered each other even before they had located their numbers. But her older sister, Se-hee... And then there was an old woman coming towards her, and she was so old that it would have been difficult for Myeong-hee to believe that anyone could reach such an age. Her posture straight and rigid, like a bamboo rod, in contrast with her aged face. This old lady, whose face bore no expression and who had come right up to the sign, hesitated for a moment, maybe in order to catch her breath, or maybe taking a good look at this woman, here, or else just practicing good manners, and then she took a chair and sat down. Her face a shade of chest-nut that would have been hard to find in Seoul, with creases so deep they might have been furrows drawn intentionally. And her frame, so thin. Fed at all well, it would have been difficult for anyone to have such a face or to look like that. Within this room, the noisy, chaotic passions that had been suppressed and were still impossible to express in words, were cracking the accumulated crusts of convention and breaking forth, and yet she was

없어…….

명희는 할 말을 하지 못해서, 그 말이 숨통을 막아서 도무지 의자에서 일어서지 못했다. 가슴에 소속기관과 이름을 붙인 표를 매단 여성 진행요원이 다가와 미소 지으며 나가시지요? 할 때까지도 명희는 일어설 수 없었다.

"편찮으십니까?"

남성 진행요원이 다가와 정중하고 사무적인 목소리로 물었다. 명희의 몸이 부르르 떨렸다. 진저리로 근육이 풀린 것일까. 새로운 긴장에 정신을 차린 것일까. 명희는 두 손으로 원탁을 누르고 힘겹게 일어서서 배낭을 짊어졌다. 그리고 무언가 훌쩍 빠져나간 듯 횡횡한 상봉장을 나섰다. 55년 기다려서 두 시간 만나고 두 시간 자유와 공백을 지난 뒤에 다시 이곳에서 만찬을 할 거였다.

명희의 혼란은 개인과 집단에 대한 보호와 억압의 제도화 이후 역사의 어느 한때 생기는 정신질환 중의 하나일지 몰랐다. 명희가 세희와 헤어진 1950년 9월 18일 이후, 열두 살 여자아이의 인생은 '이리 치이고 저리 치

only calm, and immersed in a desolate silence.

"So Myeong-hee has come."

'But where is my older sister?' This was the absurd thought that Myeong-hee was having, just at that moment. And at that moment, the old lady who resembled a bamboo rod and was now seated across from her spoke in a voice that was strange and young: "So Myeong-hee has come." But Myeong-hee was blocking those words, 'So Myeong-hee has come,' with this crust, this 'But where is my older sister?' And then the silence fell again. At certain tables, the teams of journalists from the North and those of the South had gathered and were having a small party, along with the personnel who comprised the event's staff, also from both the North and the South; sobs that could not be held in were heard from other quarters; elsewhere, there were sounds of soft laughter; from some places, there were voices with questions and voices with answers; and again and again, from here and from there, 'The General!' was heard. Myeong-hee wished that she could say, 'Older Sister'. She wanted to address this one as 'Older Sister'. But she could not look at that face, the face of this old lady whom her older sister must never ever be. Crush

였다'는 말 이외엔 달리 표현할 마땅한 말이 없었다. 그래도 살아남을 수 있었던 건 오직 깊이 감춰둔 희망, 꿈, 자부심인 세희 언니 때문이었다. 명희의 생존본능이 너무 깊이, 감쪽같이, 앙큼하게 숨겨서 방공법도 정보부도 안전기획부……도 알아낼 수 없고 찾아낼 수 없었던 희망, 꿈, 자부심이었다.

그러나 명희는 배우가 아니었다. 기다려야 하는 일이 남아서 명희를 살게 했지만 다른 역할은 할 수 없었다. 나이를 먹어 저절로 변하는 것 말고 다른 것은 하나도 가지지 않았다. 연인이 되는 것, 아내가 되는 것, 어머니가 되는 것, 할머니가 되는 것. 그런 건 할 수 없었다. 말로 할 수 없는 고통과 불행은 자기 하나로 충분해서. 자신으로 하여금 또 다른 사람을 불행하게 할 수 없었다.

처녀 시절로부터 중년에 이르기까지 애정을 고백하는 남자들이 더러 있긴 했다. 그 진심이 쓰라리게 느껴지기도 했었다. 전쟁의 와중에서 우연찮게 식모로 들어앉게 되었던 집 주인 남자, 그 남자의 동생, 그 남자의 아들까지 줄줄이 덮쳤던 기억 말고 남자와 맨살을 맞물려본 적이 없었다. 열세 살의 명희는 사타구니가 찢기

Kim Il-sung. Unification by the South. But those devious infiltrators. Et cetera. While hatred and denigration had been accumulating inside of the one nation divided by ideas, Myeong-hee had held her older sister within, to keep her from harm. Myeong-hee would not allow that those things had anything to do with her older sister, Se-hee. There must be such a world as her older sister had talked about, where no one was poor, and where there was no discrimination against anyone.

When had she put her hands on the table? Myeong-hee's hands were on the table, and they were shaking, so she hid them underneath. And it was not just her hands that were shaking. The rest of her body was shaking as well, and hard. Her body was also quite cold, and had been for some time, now.

"Older... Sister..."

Myeong-hee had wanted to say this phrase. Her voice, though, could not get out past her lips, which just moved up and down as if she were paralyzed with delirium. Then this old lady Se-hee started to open the bound kerchief that was there on the table. What was this? Maybe some part of that fifty-five years, in solid form? There were a

는 고통을 느꼈지만 그 집에서 열여섯 살까지 벙어리처럼 일만 하며 살았다. 그 집 여자들은 모두 제 몸을 황소처럼 마구 부리며 일밖에 모르는 명희를 착하다며 아꼈다. 여자의 성징인 생리는 그 집을 나와 공장에 취직한 열여덟 살 이른 봄에 시작됐다. 그날 변소에서 명희는 오래도록 울었다. 왜 우는지도 모른 채였다.

만찬까지의 두 시간을 보내려는 사람들은 온정각 휴게소 근처를 산책하거나 끼리끼리 모여 갖은 소회들을 털어놓기도 했다. 북측에서 운영하는 선술집 의자는 동이 났고 북한 물건들을 사는 사람들도 꽤 됐다. 북한의 서커스가 공연되고 있는 원형극장으로 몰려가거나 건너편 찻집으로 커피를 마시러 가는 사람들도 있었다.

명희는 여전히 혼자였다. 누구도 명희에게 말을 걸지 않았다. 명희도 곁을 주지 못했다. 화단가에 놓인 차가운 화강암에 걸터앉아 멍한 눈으로 허공을 바라보았다. 바람이, 블록을 깐 광장을 바닥부터 쓸어 올리며 뿌연 먼지를 불어 올렸다.

언니는 어디 갔지?

명희는 불현듯 사방을 둘러보았다. 55년 동안 겉모습

number of medals, similar in size to coins, a book of photos and several certificates of recognition. Myeong-hee clutched at her own fingers under the table, pullng and pressing them. They ached, and seemed about to break.

"...By the mercy of Grand Marshall Kim Il-sung and General Kim Jong-il, I have lived this well. Just look at all these medals."

The tone was not at all the one in which Se-hee had first spoken, saying 'So Myeong-hee has come,' and so what was heard was a big voice that seemed forced. Wearing Kim Jong-il badges, members of the support team were walking about, making slow circuits among the round tables with smiles on their faces. And at all of the round tables, there were people doing the same things. Myeong-hee's stomach was in pain. Just like those times when there had been attacks night and day, with the U.S. conducting air raids, when her older sister Se-hee's once hopeful face had come to be full of anxiety and she would frequently utter the words 'the American enemy', and when her own stomach would be in pain, so that she was not able to eat anything, now Myeong-hee was again sick to her stomach. She pressed at the base of her abdomen

은 늙었는데 함께 늙지 못한 딱한 감정 하나가 있었다. 그 감정 하나가 명희의 인생이었다.

등산용 배낭을 짊어진 젊은 단체여행자들이 무리지어 지나갔다.

여기가 어디지? 내가 왜 여기 있지? 아, 언니는!

명희는 얼얼했다. 눈앞이 하얘졌다가 새카매졌다. 사람들이 보이다가 없어지고 빈 벌판에 사람들이 점점이 나타나기를 되풀이했다.

언, 니, 는, 어, 디, 갔, 지?

쌀이 떨어지기 전에 돌아온다던 언니……는.

명희는 예순 여섯 살의 할머니였으나 지금 저 홀로 떨어져 앉아 뒤죽박죽인 애증의 심연에서 시달렸다. 늙어서도 벗지 못한 어린 계집아이의 옷이 명희의 살갗을 파고들어 살이 된 지 오래였다. 엉덩이가 시리고 저릴 때까지 쑥돌에 앉아 있는 것도 여기가 언니와 함께 살던 문간방 앞이라고 믿으려는 질병 같은 집착에서였다.

명희의 55년처럼, 가족을 떠나 북으로 간 피붙이를 기다리는 쪽은 남측이었다. 금강산 높은 바위 봉우리로부터, 보이지 않는 해금강 푸른 바다로부터, 곧게 뻗어

with both of her hands. Meanwhile, Se-hee went on and on, saying that her life had been a happy one, all because of the infinite love of the great Grand Marshall, Kim Il-sung, and General Kim Jong-il, and how, as one who worked for the unification and the liberation of their nation, she had been well taken care of.

"Older Sister."

Crying, Myeong-hee now addressed her as her older sister. And from Se-hee there was not a hint of a response. As if a tape recorder had been set playing, she just went on with her speech, over and over about her own heroic life and the love of the General. The round table, which could have accommodated six people, seemed terribly wide, keeping them terribly distant. As hands were seized and cheeks caressed in certain families, and as a son prostrated himself before his mother who did not see well, crews from the media of both the North and the South would rush over to get some pleasant photos, as if that was what they had been waiting for, and they would ask for the same motions to be gone through again and again. A wife from the South who had raised her only son and lived alone for more than half of a century, and her

울창한 금강산 솔숲으로부터, 깊어진 가을의 저녁 기운이 기웃거리기 시작했다. 여기저기 흩어져 낯설고 눈치보이는 감정을 다스리지 못하는 방문단의 나이 많은 사람들은 무겁거나 홀연하거나 들뜨거나 얼떨떨한 모습으로 첫 상봉을 겪은 만찬장 쪽으로 움직이기 시작했다. 오래도록 가위눌린 마음은 쉽게 원래의 것으로 돌아가지 못한 듯 보였다. 지독한 그리움은 아직도 저마다의 깊은 과거에 자취를 숨기고 있을 것이었다.

만찬장의 음식은 먹을 것이 담긴 그릇을 겹쳐놓아야 할 지경으로 가짓수가 많았다. 그러나 뜬 것들을 푸근히 가라앉히는 된장찌개, 혀에 짜르르한 김치, 볕에 잘 익은 조선간장에 담백한 간이 배고 들기름 내 그윽이 풍기는 나물 반찬은 없었다. 여기저기서 북측 억양이 기름처럼, 거품처럼 떠올랐다 꺼지곤 하였다. 술을 잔에 붓고 건배를 이끄는 인사말도 행사에 걸맞추어 순서대로 이어졌다. 전쟁과 분단, 이산의 의미가 그저 글자에 지나지 않는, 헤어진 이와 나누었던 추억이 없는 남측의 청소년들은 서둘러 음식을 먹고 자리를 떴다. 오고가고 주고받는 술은 잔치가 분명한데 분위기는 한사

husband from the North, who had married again and had many children and grand-children. These, too, could say but little to teach other. There was a son, crying for some time over the academic career he had desired for himself and had not been able to continue, having been compelled to give it up because of connections that were suspect, while the grand-son, feeling quite awkward next to his grand-father, gazed at his grand-father's medals and badges with a puzzled look.

For Myeong-hee, the two hours flew away like dust, just as they did for everyone. The people who had come from the North were the first to rise from their seats, and they received the good wishes of the families from the South, who moved automatically, like magnets, to follow them as they stepped out through the doors. Two hours later, there was to be a feast. Two hours later, they were going to meet again. In accordance with the plan.

When Se-hee stood up, Myeong-hee did not look at her, and she would not listen to what she was saying.

When those from the North had left the room, the excitement of those two hours, along with the expectation, the fear, the anger and the regret she

코 묵직하고 복잡했다.

그러나 어느 한 가족도 똑같지는 않았다. 벌써 과거를 현재로 만들어 가족의 안부를 묻고 화답하는 가족들도 있었다. 남측에서도 잘 살고 북측에서도 남다르게 '성공'한 가족들이 대개 그랬다. 아무것도 먹지 못하고 언니의 손을 잡고 우는 늙은 동생, 좀체 눈을 마주치지 않는 늙은 수절 아내, 그 슬픔과 배반감을 차마 감당하지 못해 눈치 보는 할아버지, 귀가 우중충하고 눈이 잘 보이지 않는 어머니에게 음식을 떠먹여주는 반백의 아들, 이런저런 높낮이로 웃고 우는 소리가 크고 작은 말소리에 뒤섞이고 있었다.

명희는 고개를 한쪽으로 튼 채 건배를 위해 채웠던 잔을 비운 세희를 보았다. 그리고 그 많은 음식 중에서 제육 한 점을 집어 먹는 것도 보았다. 그러나 세희가 지금 그것을 씹으며 지난 십여 년의 참혹했던 북한, 그 모진 고난의 행군시절을 떠올리는 건, 명희에겐 상상이 불가능했다. 북한의 수해와 홍수, 그리고 미국의 경제 조치 따위는 명희에게 절박했던 적이 없었다. 그래서 지금 배곯아 죽어나간 동무들이 걸려 모래알 같은 고깃

had had before was gone, vanished like a lie. Some of those from the South still could not get up from their seats, most of them with expressions of despondence, frustration, despair and grief, which created a strange tone, even as they were tempered with some of relief. Over the heaped ashes of ten thousand, or of twenty thousand. The temporary stage thrown up over one of those symbolic sites was now pulled down as though it had been nothing special, and these people, bereft of family, could not accept it as nothing special, and so they could not stand up from their seats.

Soon all the people from the North had gone out, and so all of those from the South left, and the place was emptied, but Myeong-hee could not get up from her chair.

"This is not it!"

Myeong-hee shook her head hard. If that were indeed her Older Sister, Se-hee... No, this is not it! My older sister could never have taken such a form! What, lived well? If that was my older sister Se-hee, she would have begun by telling me that she was sorry for failing to keep her promise. And then she should have commended me for having made it through well, myself. That is how she

점을 부실한 이빨로 어설피 오래도록 씹고 있는, 그 슬픔을 명희는 도저히 헤아릴 수 없었다. 그게 세희의 민족 감정으론 마냥 서글프고 한편 가당찮았다.

"한 잔 해라. 먹은 거 내리기에도…… 술기운이 보탬이 된다."

세희가 말했다. 낮고 무겁고 싸늘했다. 조국의 자주통일과 외세로부터 민족자주성을 유린당하지 않으려는 당의 방침에 헌신한 평생. 어떤 슬픔, 어떤 그리움도 그것에 우선하지 않았다. 어떤 슬픔, 어떤 그리움에도 부끄럽지 않았다.

명희는 저절로 잔을 들었다. 언니가 든 잔에 부딪쳤다.

"찬이 풍성하구나."

세희가 말했다. 명희는 안주로 생선전을 집어 들었다. 한 입 삼키기 무섭게 속이 매슥거렸다.

"명희야. 네가 내 동생이라면 민족의 자주통일 사업에 동참해야 한다. 위대한 지도자 동지……"

"언니!"

순간 명희가 세희를 부르며 똑바로 쳐다보았다. 눈에 눈물이 그렁그렁 했다.

ought to have been, my older sister Se-hee. Having missed me. Never having forgotten or failed to think of me, even for a single day. That is how my older sister should have been, no? So no, this is not it. Truly, this is not it. No, I can not forgive this...

What Myeong-hee wanted to say, she could not, and it was because these words blocked her breath that she could not rise from her chair. Even when a woman who was assisting at the event came over, wearing upon her chest a badge that gave her station and her name, and said with a smile, "Let's be on our way, please," Myeong-hee could not stand up.

"Are you not well?" asked another member of the staff, a man who had come over and who spoke with respect and formality. Myeong-hee was shaking, hard. She had been horrified, and maybe this had weakened her muscles. And then she seemed to have regained some strength, maybe because of this new tension? Myeong-hee pressed both of her hands down on the round table, rose with much effort and then pulled her bag up and onto her back. And then she went out from the now empty site of the reunion, from which it seemed that something had just departed, all of a sudden. After

"언니. 나 그런 말 들으러 여기 온 거 아니야. 난 언니를 한시도 잊은 적이 없었어. 언니가 내 언니라면 그때를 잊어선 안 되지. 내가 열두 살이었어. 미군 폭격기가 밤낮으로 떴잖아. 동네가 쑥대밭이 됐잖아. 난 어디가 어딘지 분간도 못했다고. 타다 남은 나뭇가지에 걸린 핏덩이, 내장, 살덩이 들이 뭔지, 팔다리만 떨어져 나뒹구는 게 뭔지, 죽은 어머니 가슴을 파고 우는 어린아이가 뭔지…… 미쳐서 여태 살았는데 거기 희망을 지펴준 게 언닌데."

명희는 울면서 말했다. 세희는 아무 말도 하지 않았다. 단지 깊은 한숨을 몇 번 쉬었다. 명희네 자리 뒤쪽 어디에서 노랫소리가 들려왔다. 남자 어른이 애절한 음성으로 황성옛터를 부르고 있었다. 매슥거리던 속이 뒤집힐 것 같았다. 입을 앙다물고 구역질을 가라앉히려 애썼다. 어디서는 '반갑습니다'라는 북한 가요가 들려왔다. 좁은 통로를 사이에 둔 앞쪽에서 장년의 한 남자가 자리를 박차고 일어나 몸을 비틀며 급히 바깥으로 나갔다. 세희가 자주통일만이 살길이라고 말하기 시작했다. 명희는 방금 그 남자처럼은 아니었으나 황급히 일어섰

60

fifty-five years of waiting and then a meeting of two hours together, there would now be two hours of freedom and space, and then they would be here again, for dinner.

It may be that Myeong-hee's confusion was one of those psychotic episodes found at certain points in history after some term in which there is protection for individuals or groups, as well as systematic or institutional pressure. After 18 September, 1950, when Myeong-hee and Se-hee became separated, there was a twelve year-old girl who then lived in a way that can only be described as being kicked around, this way and that way. And if she did manage to survive, this was because of her older sister Se-hee, who had been her hope, her dream and her pride, all of which she had kept hidden deep within. Moved by the instinct for life, she had hidden them so far down, so well and with such cunning that neither the Code for the Preservation of Order, the Anti-Communist Code, the National Intelligence Agency nor the National Security Planning Agency could detect or discover that hope, that dream or that pride.

Myeong-hee, however, was not an actress. What was left her was only to wait, and for this she had

다. 배 밑바닥부터 솟구쳐 오르는 구역질이 더 참아지
지 않았다.

여자 화장실은 북적거렸다. 음식을 탓하는 사람, 행사
가 지겹다고 말하는 사람, 돌아가고 싶다는 사람, 이런
게 다 저쪽의 딸라 벌이라는 사람의 말 등이 무책임하
게 섞이고 있었다. 이런 중에 급히 활명수를 찾고 우황
청심환을 구하는 사람도 있었다. 명희는 변기 앞에 쪼
그려 앉아 먹은 것을 모두 올렸다. 먹은 것 없어 쓴물까
지 넘어오는 듯하더니 이윽고 텅 빈 속이 편해졌다. 힘
겹게 일어서자 눈앞에 별이 소나기같이 쏟아졌다.

남자 화장실 앞이 왁자해졌다.

"아니 뭐 저런 게 있어! 저러고도 삼촌이야? 우리가
자기 때문에 얼마나 고생하고 살았는데 미안하단 말 한
마디 없이 뭐? 죽여 버릴 거야! 죽여야 돼!"

사람들이 몸을 가누지 못하는 그에게 달려들었다. 그
남자는 죽일 거라고 죽여야 한다고 연신 외쳤다. 한 번
의 짧은 소란은 화장실과 복도 쪽에 길고 큰 여운을 남
겼다. 명희는 몸도 마음도 지쳐서 복도에 놓인 의자에
쓰러지듯 앉아서 만찬이 끝날 때까지 들어가지 않았다.

to survive, but she could not transform herself into anything else. There was nothing else for her, and the only changes through which she could pass were those which occurred naturally, with age. For her, the evolution of becoming a lover, a wife, a mother or a grandmother had never been an option. Quite enough, the ineffable pain and the sorrow, in herself alone. She would not have other people made miserable because of her.

From the time when Myeong-hee had been a young woman until the time when she was living in middle age, there had been men who would profess their love for her. She had felt their sincerity, and it had hurt. During the war, she had become a servant in the kitchen of a house, and she had memories of being raped there by the master of the house, by his brother and by his son, one after the other, and these memories were the only ones she had of her naked body with a man. At thirteen years old, Myeong-hee had known that tearing pain at her crotch, but then she had just continued to work, and to live in that house as if she were mute, until she turned sixteen. The women of the house had regarded Myeong-hee as an asset, since she did nothing but work and made her body to

그런데 이상했다. 명희는 북의 언니가 만나기를 희망한다는 말을 들은 이후 이날 밤 처음으로 깊은 잠을 잤다. 두 시간의 만찬을 끝내고 버스로 숙소에 돌아와 씻지도 못하고 침대에 쓰러졌었다.

이튿날 아침, 비가 내렸다. 여태 명희를 사로잡았던 언니가 눈앞에서 사라지고 비안개에 젖어 고즈넉한 장전항이 바라보였다. 굵지 않은 빗줄기에 젖은 가을 풍경은 서늘하고도 아늑했다. 어제는 이곳으로 왔고 내일은 이곳을 떠날 것이었다. 오전엔 개별 상봉이 있고 점심을 먹은 뒤, 삼일포로 나들이를 갈 것이었다. 명희는 이런 일정들을 머리에 그리며 언니를 비웃고, 버렸다. 마치 55년을 게워내듯 해일처럼 솟구치던 지독한 환멸의 감정도, 지금은 얼핏 우스울 지경이었다. 모두 거짓말 같았다. 55년조차 없던 세월 같았다. 행여 길에 떨어뜨릴까, 누가 훔쳐갈까, 여미고 또 여민 천 달러. 주지 말까? 야비한 맘도 스쳐 지나갔다. 식모로 가정부로 식당으로 공사판으로 병원으로 돌아다니며 못 배우고 가난하고 피붙이 없는 여자가 할 수 있는 일은 무엇이든지 다 했지만 불광동에 스무 평짜리 다세대주택 한 칸

endure like that of a bull. Menstruation, the symbol of the woman, began for her in the spring, when she was eighteen years old, when she had left that house and gotten a job in a factory. Myeong-hee wept that day, sobbing in the bathroom. She could not yet understand, though, what it was that made her cry.

To pass the two hours they had until the feast, some people wandered about the grounds of this On-jeong Gak Rest Area, and some gathered into groups to exchange their opinions on a variety of subjects. All of the seats were full at the tavern, which was run by North Korea, and there were quite a few people making purchases, buying North Korean products. Some people moved along to the amphitheater, where a circus was being presented, while others had gone into the café opposite for coffee.

Myeong-hee was still by herself. No one spoke to her. Nor could Myeong-hee open herself to others. She just sat there, on some cold granite that had been placed near a garden of flowers, her eyes empty and staring out upon nothing. The square, paved with concrete blocks, was caressed by the

마련한 게 십 년이 못 됐다. 곗돈도 떼이고 불쌍하고 급한 사람에게 빌려준 돈 받아본 기억이 별로 없었다. 게다가 사기 분양에도 걸린 적이 있어 벌어서 제 몸 위해 사치한 적 없고 일가친척 모르고 살아 누구 밑으로 들어간 돈도 없었지만 목돈으로 쥐지 못했다. 사람 말을 그저 믿어, 뭐가 사기인지 거짓인지 분간할 줄 몰랐다.

추운 북쪽에서 세희 언니 한겨울 춥지 않게 나라고 마련한 내의는 단체 선물로 모아졌다. 정해진 개별 상봉장. 호텔의 객실 한 칸씩이 배정됐다. 문 한 짝 사이로 난 복도에서 저벅거리는 발자국 소리가 자주 들렸다. 아, 얼마 만인가. 일흔 줄과 예순 줄의, 부모자식 같은 자매는 도무지 입을 열지 못했다. 세희는 할 만큼 해서인지, 동생에게 조급히 주입하려 애쓰던 민족자주통일의 혁명과업에 대해 말하지 않았다. 몸에도 잡혔을 것 같은 얼굴과 몸과 손의 주름 사이로 비리고 서늘한 슬픔과 회한의 눈물이 저릿저릿 비끼는 듯했다.

"자식은 몇이나 됐냐."

두 시간의 개별 상봉. 말없이 반 시간도 넘게 흘려보낸 뒤에 세희가 낮고 젖은 목소리로 물었다. 무안당한

wind, which moved up from its lower end, blowing clouds of dust up and around.

'But where is my older sister?'

Myeong-hee suddenly looked about her, in every direction. Her features had grown old in the course of fifty-five years, but there was within her a certain melancholy that had not aged. And that melancholy was Myeong-hee's life.

A group of young tourists with hiking packs on their backs passed by.

'Where am I? What am I doing here? Ah, where's my older sister?'

Myeong-hee was getting confused. All that was before her eyes became white, and then it went black. People came into view, people disappeared, and then there were people here and there against an empty field, and then it all repeated.

'But. Where. Is. My. Older. Sister?'

My older sister, who... said she would be back before the rice was gone.

Myeong-hee was a sixty-six year-old old woman, but she sat alone, off to the side, and she suffered the pain of a complicated abyss of love and hate. Although she had grown old, she had never been able to remove the clothing of a little girl,

속 좁은 아이처럼 내내 고개를 숙이고 있던 명희는 불현듯 고개를 추켜들었다. 놀란 눈빛이었으나 표정은 굳어 보였다. 세희가 그 얼굴을 바라보며 모처럼 할머니다운 미소를 머금었다. 그런 동안에도 명희는 언니의 물음을 삭히지 못해 울화로 굳은 표정을 풀지 못했다.

"손자도 봤겠구나."

세희가 여전한 목소리로 말했다. 순간 명희의 얼굴에 모멸이 지나갔다. 세희가 생수병을 비틀어 마개를 열고 잔에 물을 따랐다. 세희가 마른 입술과 입 안을 축이는 동안 명희의 입술이 파르르 떨고 있었다. 입 안에서 까슬대고 고물대던 말들이 결국 샜다.

"자식이 뭐래?"

명희는 빈정거림을 감추지 못했다. 순간 세희의 검은 얼굴에 더욱 검은 그림자가 덮였다.

"언니 사는 데선 손자라는 게 하늘에서 떨어져? 별나기도 해라."

명희는 다시 물 잔을 들어 꿀꺽거리는 소리를 내며 마시는 세희에게 한 번도 뱉어본 적이 없는 야비하고 가혹한 말을 뱉었다.

which had long ago become fused with her skin. Sitting thus on the stone, even as her buttocks became cold and then numb, she suffered a persistent confusion, in which she perceived this place as if it were out in front of the spare room where she had once lived with her sister.

These people who were waiting for this reunion with their own flesh and blood, members of their own lines, just as Myeong-hee had waited for fifty-five years, were the ones from the South, waiting for those who had left them and gone to the North. Now, from the high rocky peaks of the Geum-gang Mountains, from the blue sea that extended out beyond Hae Geum-gang, the island that lay out of sight, from the Geum gang Mountains' pine trees, tall and mighty, the atmosphere of an evening in the depths of autumn began to peer through. Now scattered about, the old people in this group of visitors, not able to calm their strange emotions or compulsive anxiety, started to move towards the site of the feast, a place of which they now had some experience, from the earlier encounter, some looking heavy, some of them abrupt, some excited and others held in shock. Maybe the heart, after such a term of delirium and

"난 언니가 기다리라고 한 날부터 이제껏 인생을 단 한 발짝도 떼어놓지 못했어."

명희가 입술을 깨물었다.

"언니는 어땠는지 몰라도 난 언니를 만나면 하고 싶은 게 딱 한 가지 있었어. 언니를 피나게 때려주고 싶었어. 그런데…… 나한텐 언니가 없었네. 그걸 몰랐어. 나이를 못 먹어서."

명희는 훌쩍거렸다. 눈물 콧물을 수건에 닦았다.

"언니는 잘나서 나한테 자랑이 늘어졌지만 난 언니한테 보여줄 것도 자랑할 것도 없어. 언니의 자랑이 아무리 잘났어도 나한테 쓸모가 없으니 못 받아줘."

명희는 자신이 무슨 말을 하는지 알지 못했다. 그저 터진 봇물처럼 말이 쏟아져 나왔다. 살아오면서 이래 본 적이 없었다.

"난 기다려야 하는 줄 알았으니까. 그거밖에 하고 싶은 게 없었으니까. 그런데 알았어. 나한텐 기다렸던 언니가 없다는 걸. 그걸 알게 됐어. 죽을 때 눈이나 감고 죽으라고…… 알게 됐네."

명희의 눈의 열기는 물기에 젖어 더욱 번들거렸다. 세

paralysis, could not get easily back into its original state. There would always be that yearning that would not be ignored, hiding in the depths of each one's past.

So numerous were the dishes then, there at the feast, that there were plates of food which had to be set on top of others. However, there was no bean paste soup, bringing calm with its warmth, no *kim-chi* that would sting the tongue, no vegetable dishes giving a subtle scent of perilla oil and seasoned just right with soy sauce that had been well fermented in the sun. Throughout the place, the North Korean accent would appear and then be dispersed, like oil or like foam. Cups were filled, toasts were made and one salute after another was given, all according to plan. For the teenagers from the South, this war, the division of the nation and the separation of families meant no more than the mere words themselves, and they shared none of the memories of those from whom they had been separated, so they just ate quickly and left the place. The drinks being offered and accepted suggested festivity, but the mood was still heavy and complicated.

But the families were not all the same. Some

희의 등이 흔들리고 있었다. 명희는 마음껏 비웃었다. 비웃으며 주머니에서 천 달러가 든 봉투를 꺼내 놓았다. 오백 달러 정도가 적당할 거라는 말을 들었지만 명희가 주고 싶은 건 그것의 천배 만배였다. 하얀 봉투에 적힌 검정 글씨들. 그립고 그리운 언니께, 라는 글자가 봉투 위에서 둥실둥실 떴다.

명희는 세희가 떨리는 손길로 봉투를 집어 들 때, 자리에서 일어났다. 문밖은 벌써 어수선했다. 문이 꼭꼭 닫힌 방도 있었지만 활짝 열린 방도 있었다. 주어진 상봉 시간은 아직 반 시간이나 남아 있었다. 이곳에서 나가 함께 마지막 식사인 점심을 먹고 삼일포 나들이를 하면 끝이었다. 내일 아침 작별은 오전 열 시였다.

삼십 분 후면 함께 만나 점심을 먹을 텐데 버스에 오르는 북측 피붙이를 한 번 더 보려고 차창이 잘 보이는 곳에서 누구는 손을 흔들고 누구는 버스로 이동하려는 혈육의 불편한 걸음을 부축했다. 북측에서 마련한 잔치 같은 점심식사. 그러나 초조감이 긴장감에 뒤섞여 야릇한 잔치 분위기를 자아냈다. 삼일포 나들이에선 마지막으로 사진을 찍고 마지막으로 손을 잡고 볼에 볼을 맞

families were already making the past the present, everyone asking and answering about the lives of the others. So it was with families who had prosperous and comfortable lives in the South, and whose relatives had achieved considerable success with their lives in the North. As an older brother who could not eat held his sister's hand and cried, and that old woman who had remained a proper wife could not make eye contact with her husband, the old man overwhelmed with shame brought on by her grief and her sense of having been betrayed, and the gray haired son was putting food into the mouth of his mother, who was hard of hearing and had poor eye-sight, the sounds of laughing and crying in various tones were mixed up among the sounds of conversation, loud and quiet.

With her head turned aside, Myeong-hee saw Se-hee drain a cup that had been filled for a toast. She had also seen how it was the meat that she would take up and eat, from among that multitude of dishes. But it was impossible for Myeong-hee to imagine just what it was that Se-hee must have recalled from the past decade of hard times in North Korea, which had been a time of extreme privation.

대는 사람들이 많았다. 하지만 명희는 언니와 함께 걷지 못했다. 아침과는 달리, 공연한 뜨거운 울음이 자꾸만 목을 타고 치솟아 이런 격정이 부담스럽고 싫었다. 세희도 그런 명희를 붙잡지 않았다. 그림 같은 정적이 감도는 고요하고 정갈한 삼일포. 그 주위의 바위에 기대앉기도 하고 걷기도 하면서 명희는 무엇엔가 마비되어가기 시작했다. 어제 같은 야릇한 평화, 안도감, 개운함은 거짓말 같았다. 밤이 깊도록 잠을 이루지 못했다. 이게 꿈인가? 현실인가? 연극인가? 자꾸만 허공에 질문했다.

날밤을 새워 얼굴이 부석한 명희. 다른 사람들에게서도 어제의 들뜬 분위기는 지워져 있었다. 남북의 이산가족이 처음 만났던 그 자리에서 짧은 작별의 시간이 주어졌다. 첫날 밤, 남은 가족에게 연좌제라는 고통을 준 삼촌을 죽이겠다던 그 사람은 고요했다. 말이 많던 딸들, 동생들, 모두 숙연했다. 잘 살아라. 건강하게 지내자. 통일이 되면 만나자, 모두 공소(空疎)했다.

갑자기 뭉텅 주어졌던 시간. 마치 성냥불 같았다. 이제 손끝이 타들어가게 위태롭게 남은 시간. 북측 사람

To Myeong-hee, there had been nothing urgent in the floods of North Korea, despite the damage they had done, or in the United States' economic embargo. So Myeong-hee could not have understood the sorrow that had been suffered by Se-hee, who now struggled on with her weak teeth to chew this meat, though it tasted like sand, because she felt guilty about her comrades who had died of starvation. And this did cause Se-hee some pain, though there was no good reason for it.

"Have a drink. To wash down what we ate... A little alcohol helps." These were Se-hee's words. They were low, heavy and cold. Her whole life, dedicated to the party's insistence on autonomy and demands for unification, which strove to render the nation independent and to keep it from violation by foreign powers. No suffering or yearning had ever been given greater importance than these points. Therefore, she was never ashamed or afraid of sorrow or yearning of any kind.

Myeong-hee lifted her cup by herself. Her cup touched the cup held by her sister.

"Such a lot of dishes," Se-hee said. Myeong-hee picked with her chopsticks at a fried fish filet, a complement to her drink. As soon as she had tak-

들을 태우고 떠날 버스는 줄지어 서 있고 사람들은 자기 차를 찾아 버스에 올랐다. 그중 세희도 그렇게 버스에 올랐다. 아직 명희는 아무렇지 않았다. 이별은 오래 겪은 익숙한 것이어서, 이별이 뭔지 순간 둔해졌다.

떠날 준비를 끝낸 버스는 세상에 둘도 없는 침묵의 덩어리였다. 사람들은 차창에 매달렸고 버스에 탄 사람은 차창을 열어 손을 내밀고 휘젓고 고개를 빼 두리번거렸다. 어디선가 어머니! 오빠! 여보! 아버지! 삼촌! 비명이 울리기 시작했다. 발을 동동 구르는 어른, 주저앉은 어른, 휠체어에 앉아 손을 흔들다 얼굴을 감싸는 할아버지…… 그 사이로 명희가 '언니'를 외마디로 외쳐 부르기 시작했다. 언니한테 뭘 잘못한 게 있었는데, 언니! 잘못했어, 내가 잘못했어!! 이 말을 꼭 해야 하는데, 이렇게 헤어져선 안 되는데…… 열두 살의 명희가, 예순일곱 살의 명희가, 아무리 발버둥치고 넋두리해도 또다시 놓친 언니를 붙잡을 수는 없었다.

『건너편 섬』, 자음과모음, 2014

en a bite of it, she felt sick.

"Myeong-hee. If you are my younger sister, then you ought to participate in our efforts towards national independence and unification. The Great Leader, Comrade—"

"Older Sister!"

Myeong-hee stared right at her then, as she addressed Se-hee. Her eyes were filled with tears.

"Older Sister, I didn't come here to listen to that. I never forgot you, not for a moment. And if you were my older sister, then you shouldn't have forgotten that time. I was twelve years old. The U.S. military was flying over, and there were air raids day and night. The whole area was in ruins. I never even knew one place from another. Or what intestines hanging in the branches of a burned up tree were. Or what that was, rolling around without any arms or legs. Or what that infant was, crying and hidden at the bosom of its dead mother... I lived through insanity, and you were my only hope."

Myeong-hee wept as she spoke. Se-hee didn't say a word. She sighed several times, and that was all. A song was heard, coming from over beyond Myeong-hee's place. Some man was singing 'Hwang Seong, the Ruins of the Old Imperial Site' in melancholic tones. It seemed the nausea in the stomach was being stirred up. Pressing her lips together, she tried to hold it down. And then the North Korean song, "Well Met", was heard. Up at the front, along which there ran a narrow aisle, a middle-aged man shot up from his chair, turned himself around and made a swift departure. Se-hee started talking about how unified independence was the only path for survival. Myeong-hee got to her feet, not quite as the man had done, but quickly. The nausea that was rushing up from the depths of her stomach was more than she could bear.

The women's rest-room was busy. As someone complained about the food, someone else was saying that the event itself was boring, and another likewise expressed a desire to leave, while another one said the whole thing was just a way for the North to get some U.S. dollars, et cetera, all of the words getting mixed up with the others, with no-one taking responsibility. Also, in the midst of all this, there were some going for tonics supposed to aid digestion, and some going for their lenitive medicine. Myeong-hee sank down in front of a toilet and threw up everything she had eaten. Because she had not eaten very much, a thin acidic liquid came up as well, and then once her stomach was empty, she seemed to feel better. As she rose with a struggle, stars fell like a heavy rain before her eyes.

Outside of the men's room, there was some real commotion.

"No, but what the hell?! What, like that, and that's an uncle? Does he understand what we've been through—how much we suffered, because of him? And he doesn't even say he's sorry? I want to kill him! I've got to—I've just got to kill that guy!" People rushed over to this man, who was not able to steady himself. Over and over, he shouted that he had to kill the other. The moment of turmoil was brief, but its effects were large and lingered on for some time, there in the restrooms and the corridor. Tired, in a state of physical exhaustion and emotional fatigue, Myeong-hee collapse upon a bench in the corridor and sat there, not going back until the feast was over.

It was strange, though. That night Myeong-hee slept very deep, for the first time since she had heard that her older sister wanted to see her. When the two hour feast was over, she came back to the hotel by bus and fell on the bed without even washing.

The next morning, there was rain. The older sister was gone, so after being held as her captive for
all of this time, Myeong-hee looked out over the
Jang-jeon Port, which seemed lonesome, wet with
the rain and the fog. The fall scenery, dampened
by showers that had not been very heavy, looked
cool, and yet it made her feel warm and secure. It
had been only the day before that she had come to
this place, and she would leave here on the following day. The individual sessions would be held
in the morning, and after lunch, they would visit the
lake, Sam-il Po. She went over the schedule in her
head, and then she laughed at her sister and just
tossed her away. And it felt as though she must
have vomited those fifty-five years, as the strong
sense of disillusionment which had flooded over
her like a tidal wave now somehow seemed funny,
as well. Everything seemed to be a lie. It seemed
that those fifty-five years of her life had never occurred. A thousand dollars, guarded and kept close
for fear of its being dropped on the ground, or
stolen. 'Perhaps I'll not give it to her?' For a moment, she even passed through this harsh state of
mind. Doing everything that a woman could do

without money, relatives or education, serving in homes and in restaurants, and holding jobs at construction sites and in a hospital, as well, she had not been able to get her own place—a twenty *pyeong* section of a divided house in the district of Bul-gwang—until less than ten years earlier. When she had invested with others, the funds had been lost, and while she had made loans to those without when they were in urgent situations, she had never had much experience of getting that money back. And all of this was in addition to being taken in a real estate fraud, so that even if she never treated herself with any luxury, and while there were in her life no relatives on whom she might have spent her money, she had never been able to build up a sum of any size. She fell easily for whatever people told her, never able to discern deceit or detect a lie.

The set of long under-wear that Myeong-hee had had to prepare for Se-hee, so that she would not be so cold in the Northern winter, was now taken, sets being collected to be distributed all together, as a gift. The appointed site of the individual sessions. Each party was given its own chamber, among the rooms of the hotel. The mutter of foot-steps was a frequent sound, coming from the hall-way, from which they were separated by a door. "Ah, how long has it been?" Looking like a mother and daughter, though one was in her seventies and the other in her sixties, the two sisters were only just able to open their mouths. Se-hee did not speak of the revolutionary struggle for the nation's independent unification now, evidently having satisfied herself with her frantic earlier efforts to pour these things into her sister. Between the wrinkles that lined her face and hands and maybe the rest of her body, a cold and odious sorrow seemed to show itself, along with tears of regret, in a fleeting tremor,

"How many children do you have?"

The individual session, two hours. Half of an hour had been passed without words, and then Se-hee had asked this question, in a voice that was weak and moist. Myeong-hee, who had been holding her head down like a stubborn child that has been scolded, now picked her head right up. There was surprise in her eyes, and her face was like stone. Seeing that expression, Se-hee now gave her a grand-mother's smile, which was for her quite unwonted. Still, Myeong-hee could not allow her older sister's question, and instead of falling back, her features grew yet harder.

"And there must be some grand-children?" said Se-hee, in the same voice. At that, contempt rushed over Myeong-hee's face. Se-hee twisted the cap of a water bottle, opened it and poured some water into a cup. While Se-hee moistened her lips and her mouth, which had grown dry, Myeong-hee's own lips were shaking. At last, the coarse words that had been in motion now found their way out.

"What are children?"

Myeong-hee could not suppress the impulse towards sarcasm. Darker shades fell upon the already dark face of Se-hee.

"Where you live, grand-children, they fall from the sky? What a strange place."

Myeong-hee went on, speaking as she never had, in words harsh and mean, against the sound of Se-hee sipping at the water from the cup she held.

"From the day you told me to wait and even until now, I have never taken a single step into my life."

Myeong-hee bit her lips.

"I don't how it was for you, but there was only

one thing I wanted to do, were I ever to see you again. I wanted to strike my older sister, and to make her bleed. But then... I never had any older sister. But I didn't know it. Because I was never able to grow up."

Myeong-hee was starting to cry. She wiped with a hand-kerchief at her tears and her nose.

"Sure, being so great, you can just talk and talk, making your boasts, but me, I have nothing, nothing to show you, nothing of which to boast to my older sister. And since your boasting does nothing for me, as great as it might be, I just can't stand it."

Myeong-hee was not quite aware of what she was saying. The words just poured out, as a dammed reservoir may break through. Never before had she been like this.

"I thought I had to wait. And I had no other wishes, only to wait. But now I know. I was waiting for an older sister, but there was no older sister. I know that now. So when I die, I will be able to close my eyes... now that I know."

The fire in Myeong-hee's eyes grew moist, and so it came to shine the more. Se-hee's back shook. Myeong-hee let herself laugh as she liked. Scoffing, she took out from her pocket the envelope that held the one thousand dollars. They had been told that five hundred dollars might suffice, but Myeong-hee now wished she were able to give a thousand times more, and ten thousand times more. Black letters written on the white envelope. 'For my Older Sister, so far and so dear' they said, the letters floating up from the envelope.

When Se-hee, with a shaking hand, had picked up the envelope, Myeong-hee rose from her seat. On the other side of the door, it was already getting noisy. Some of the rooms were still closed, but there were others that were now wide open. About half of an hour remained of the time that had been reserved for these sessions. Afterwards, there would be lunch, their last meal together, they would visit the lake, Sam-il Po, and that would be it. They were to bid 'fare well' at ten, the next morning.

For lunch, they would meet again in thirty minutes, but some people were out there, waving their arms where they would be seen from the windows of the bus, in order to have another good look at their Northern relatives who had boarded, while some others helped their relatives to make their way out to the bus on difficult steps. Lunch, another feast, prepared by the North. With a certain tension, though, and with anxiety, the atmosphere at the feast was strange. On the visit to Sam-il Po, there were many people taking their final pictures, holding hands for the last time and pressing their cheeks together. But Myeong-hee could not bring herself to walk along with her older sister. This was in contrast with the morning, as she now bore a burden of explosive emotions, with burning sobs surging in her throat, and it was hard, and she hated it. Nor did Se-hee make any effort to stay with her. The atmosphere at Sam-il Po, calm, just as it should have been, like that of a painted picture. As Myeong-hee reclined against the rocks, and as she walked around near the lake, a paralysis began to come over her. Yesterday, she had felt refreshed, but now she felt it had been a lie, along with that peculiar peace and that sense of relief. Well into the depths of the night, then, she was not able to sleep. A dream? Reality? A charade? Again and again, she sent these questions out into the void.

The whole night, Myeong-hee without sleep, and now a weary face. And from others, the excitement of the previous day was now erased. At the place where these families, divided between the North and the South, had met first, they were given a short time to bid each other fare-well. He was silent, now, the one who had been shouting on the first day about how he wanted to kill his uncle for the persecution the family had lived through because of their dark political connections. For the talkative daughters, for those younger siblings and all of them, it was somber. "Live well," they said. "Let's live on in good health. And we'll get together again, when it's unified." But everything was empty, and none of it was right.

A solid mass of time, given all at once. It was like the light from a match. The time left, almost at the tips of the fingers, the fire, the danger. The buses that would take those of the North were standing there, in a row, and people found their buses and boarded. Se-hee was among them, and so she got on her bus, too. Yet Myeong-hee was okay. Separation was an experience she had known for such a long time that she had become accustomed, so she was not sensitive to it.

Never in this world could there be another body of silence such as that of those buses, ready to depart. There were people reaching up towards the windows of the buses, while people inside opened the windows to put their hands out, put their heads out and look around. There were shouts, and they resounded. "Mother!" "Brother!" "Dearest!" "Father!" "Uncle!" An old person, feet stomping on the ground, someone else down in a crouch, there on the ground, an old man sitting in a wheel-chair, his hands shaking, his face covered with his hands... Among them, Myeong-hee started to shout, "Older Sister!" She had been unjust to her older sister; she needed to acknowledge this; they could not be separated, not like this... Myeong-hee, twelve years old, sixty-seven year-old Myeong-hee, she would struggle with this, and how hard, and she would grieve, but she could not catch hold of her now, the sister she had now lost again.

Translated by Chang Chung-hwa and Andrew James Keast

해설

Afterword

분단의 맺힌 감성을 해원(解冤)하는

고명철 (문학평론가)

한국 현대소설사에서 여성의 주체적 시각으로 여성을 에워싼 안팎의 문제를 날카롭게 포착한 작가로서 이경자를 꼽지 않을 수 없다. 무엇보다 오랫동안 한국사회를 무겁게 짓눌러온 가부장제의 남성중심주의로부터 비롯한 억압적 근대와 맞선 치열한 그의 글쓰기는 페미니즘의 새 지평을 열어젖혔다 해도 과언이 아니다. 그의 소설에서 때로는 예각적으로, 때로는 섬세하게, 때로는 포용적으로 다뤄지는 여성의 문제는 단지 여성 자체의 해방에 초점을 맞춘 게 아니라 궁극적으로 여성의 해방을 넘어선 인간의 해방과 인간의 구원을 향한 문학적 진실을 추구한다. 따라서 이경자의 소설 세계를

To Resolve the Anguish Inflicted by a Nation Divided

Ko Myeong-cheol (literary critic)

Given any familiarity with the history of modern Korean fiction, one would have to consider Lee Kyung-ja among those who have best captured both the interior problems women face and the exterior problems by which women are surrounded, understanding and presenting these experiences from a woman's point of view. There is no exaggeration in claiming that Lee's intense writing has been responsible for vast expansions of and new horizons for feminism; now engaged in a more open resistance to the oppressive forces of modern times, Lee began her career with reactions against the andro-centric culture created by

협소한 차원의 페미니즘으로 가둬 놓을 수 없다.

이 같은 면모는「언니를 놓치다」에서 여실히 읽을 수 있다.「언니를 놓치다」는 한국 현대소설의 주요한 주제 중 하나인 분단의 문제에 초점을 맞춘 것으로, 분단 이산의 상처가 여성 주체의 시각으로 내밀히 다뤄지고 있다. 그동안 한국 현대소설사에서 숱하게 다뤄진 분단서사와 달리 이경자의 분단서사는 감상적 낭만주의로 포괄할 수 있는 통일 추구의 서사와도 거리를 둘 뿐만 아니라, 분단 이데올로기의 이념적 질곡과 모순에 대한 사회과학적 상상력의 서사와도 거리를 두고, 그밖에 최근 붐을 일으키고 있는 디아스포라와 탈식민주의 서사와도 거리를 둔다. 이경자의 분단서사는 분단의 고통을 앓고 있는 이산가족의 삶에 밀착함으로써 그들을 짓누르며 그들의 삶을 헤집어 놓았던 정치사회적 이념의 대립과 갈등으로부터 비롯한 상처와 아픔의 속살을 어루만지는 '동감(同感)의 글쓰기'를 보인다. 특히 이 소설을 통해 작가는 이산가족 당사자인 두 여성의 삶에 깊숙이 새겨진 분단의 상처를 응시함으로써 분단 문제를 온전히 이해하고 진정으로 극복하기 위해서는 어떠한 노력이 절실한지를 한반도의 주민 모두가 성찰하도록 한다.

the patriarchal order whose severe restrictions have confined Korean society for ages. The concerns which Lee's stories have always addressed—with frequent exercise of precision, delicacy and tolerance—are indeed those of women, and yet the intention or hope that may be called the focus of her work has grown beyond any emancipation that reaches out only to women, moving instead towards a literary truth that might liberate all of humanity, for whom it might serve as universal salvation. Thus the fiction of Lee Kyung-ja has refused to be bound within the straits of any feminism that is narrow or exclusive.

This comprehensive quality is to be found easily and with clarity in the story, "Losing a Sister". While the focus of "Losing a Sister" is the problematic division of the country between North and South, a prominent subject in modern Korean literature, Lee considers the wounds inflicted by this national disintegration from an individual woman's perspective, through the rather intimate or confidential account of a woman's personal experience. In contrast with those narrative descriptions of the country's division that have appeared in modern Korean fiction with some frequency, Lee Kyung-ja's version of

이와 관련하여, 이경자가 「언니를 놓치다」에서 주목하는 것은 한반도의 남과 북으로 분단된 이후 각 체제의 분단 이데올로기의 폭압 아래 일상이 온통 지배당할 수밖에 없는 극한의 자기소외를 넘어 자기파괴로 치달은 삶의 상처다.

   여기에는 낯선 곳에서 어린 자신을 홀로 남겨둔 채 사라진 언니에게 맺힌 분노와 그리움, 허탈감이 뒤섞인 채 뒤죽박죽 정리 안 된 분단의 상처들이 언제 치유될지 기약할 수 없는 고통으로 살아남은 자에게 고스란히 남아 있는 분단의 현재적 고통이 있다. 여기서 우리는 분단 이산가족의 내면에 흐르고 있는 "애증의 심연"에서 솟구치는 그 어떠한 것보다 순결무구한 '그리움'의 심경을 가볍게 보아 넘길 수 없다. 꿈에 그리던 이산가족을 상봉하는 자리에서도 북쪽의 체제를 선전하는 데 여념이 없는 언니의 모습을 보며 분단의 현재적 고통은 결코 관념이 아닌 엄연한 현실이라는 것을 동생은 뼈저리게 느낀다. 남측의 동생에게 중요한 것은 북측의 언니로부터 언니가 투철한 공산주의자로서 얼마나 북쪽에서 잘 살고 있는지 그 안녕을 듣고 싶은 게 아니다. 그보다 한국전쟁이 일어난 전쟁의 복판에서 어린 동생을

the rupture works at some distance from mere sentimental or romantic desire for unification, from academic, sociological theories about ideological obstacles, from the abstract irony inherent in the ideology of any faction and from the conventions established by other accounts of the phenomenon of diaspora and other post-colonial stories, all of which have been well received in recent years. As Lee's work creates such intimate connections to the lives within those families to whom the division of the country has brought pain, these stories of dissolution present a "literature of sympathy", taking one to the interior of the wounds and the pain inflicted by oppressive hostility between antagonistic social and political positions, which threw so many lives into utter chaos. In this story especially, what we see is the writer's examination of a broken country's wounds as these have been deep into the lives of two women, within whose own family the fracture is an essential element, raising questions for anyone on the Korean peninsula about the efforts through which we just might reach a thorough and functional understanding of this problem of a nation divided and then recover.

In accordance with these ideas, then, Lee con-

홀로 남겨두고 떠난 언니로부터 최소한 용서를 받고 싶었으며, 바로 그 헤어짐의 시점에서 순결한 두 영혼이 진정한 만남을 갖고 싶은 것이다. 그래야만 동생은 분단의 현실에서 겪은 온갖 삶의 상처 속에서 자기파괴로 치달은 자신을 구원할 수 있는 길이 모색될 수 있다. 하지만 안타깝게도 언니는 상봉 내내 분단 이데올로기에 친친 옭매어 있었다. 동생의 "이건 아니야!"와 "언, 니, 는, 어, 디, 갔, 지?"란 독백은 이와 같은 분단의 엄연한 현실이 압축돼 있다. 뿐만 아니라 이러한 언니의 처지를 진심으로 이해하지 못한 채, 게다가 언니의 내면에 자리한 동생과 다른 분단의 상처를 따뜻하게 어루만져주지 못한 채, 일방적으로 자신의 넋두리를 늘어놓은 데 대한 동생의 자조(自嘲)의 심경이야말로 21세기 분단의 시대를 살고 있는 우리가 깊이 성찰해야 할 분단의 과제이다.

이처럼 한국문학의 분단서사는 이경자의 「언니를 놓치다」를 통해 한층 성숙해지고 풍요로워졌다고 말할 수 있다. 21세기의 분단서사는 분단 현실에 대한 상투적 관심과 당위적 차원의 통일지상주의를 경계하면서 이산가족을 억압하고 있는 분단의 맺힌 감성을 해원(解冤)

centrates in "Losing a Sister" on the damage done to personal life, after the division of the Korean peninsula into a northern half and a southern half, through the oppression of the divisive ideology behind the systems of either faction, once that had come to dominate the basic conceptions of what was normal, so that one would first become terribly estranged from the self and then fall into a course of self-destruction.

Here there is pain, in the present, bestowed by the country's internal conflict without mitigation upon this one who has remained; these wounds were not to be eliminated through separation, and no-one can promise eventual recovery from the pain born by this one, here in this place that has become a foreign land, lost in a confusion of anger, yearning and apathy towards the older sister who had deserted her, a child alone, and vanished. We must give more than a glance at this heart, so pure, "yearning" and ready to burst out from the "abyss of love and hatre" that runs deep through the interior of the families in this country. At the site where the gathering of divided families of which she had dreamed is now taking place, the younger sister, Se-hee looks on as her older

하는 노력이 절실히 요구된다. 이 일을 작가 이경자는

그 특유의 분단서사로 실천하고 있다.

sister, Myeong-hee, preaches with energetic per-
sistence in support of the North Korean regime,
and she feels the enduring pain of the breach in
her country, not as an idea but as a reality that will
not be denied. This younger sister has no interest
in listening to what her older sister, come from the
North, has to say about the comfortable life she has
enjoyed as a devout North Korean communist. What
she had hoped to hear instead was, in a moment of
true contact with her older sister, as in an encounter between two pure souls, some confession of
regret from the older sister, who had abandoned
her, the younger sister, where battles of the Korean War were raging all around. For this younger
sister, Myeong-hee, drawn into self-destruction by
the various wounds inflicted upon her life by the
circumstances of internal hostility within the nation,
there might have been some chance of finding the
way to salvation, had such a moment occurred. She
was not so fortunate, though, as the encounter
proved the perverse rigidity with which the ideology of national division was held by her older sister,
who remained obstinate throughout. As the
younger sister mumbles to herself, saying "This is
not it!" and "Where. Is. My. Older. Sister?" we catch

the condensed essence of those circumstances, not to be denied, of the divided nation. Moreover, she only moans about herself, without regard for anyone else; she never quite understands her older sister's situation, never quite reaches, as she might with a warm touch, those wounds, set deep within her older sister and so different from the older sister, herself, inflicted like her own by the conflict within their country, and the laughter she then directs at herself suggests that a nation divided implies a responsibility for serious reflection, as we are responsible for asking serious questions about life at this stage of the twenty-first century, an age of a nation divided.

Therefore, we can say that with Lee Kyung-ja's "Losing a Sister", the Korean literary narrative of the nation divided has become more mature and more substantial. Efforts must be made so that this narrative of division in the twenty-first century will remain free from the conservative interests of that division's own established institutions, and they must be made with such strength and such intensity as are called for by their mission, which is unification, working to resolve the anguish created by the separation through which so many families have had to suffer in this separated country. That struggle is the work practiced by Lee Kyung-ja, with her unique narrative voice.

비평의 목소리

Critical Acclaim

그 누구보다 한국소설사에서 래디컬한 여성주의 문제의식의 서사지평을 객토해 온 작가 이경자에게 기존 여성주의—가부장으로서 남성이 소유해 온 사회적 권력을 쟁취하려는 '투쟁적 여성주의'—는 자족할 지상의 가치가 아니다. 이경자가 꿈꾸는 또 다른 여성주의는 이러한 '투쟁적 여성주의'를 넘어선 그래서 담대하고 포용적인 우주적 모성성으로 일체의 갈등과 대립 및 배제와 증오를 감싸 안아 그것의 경계를 평화적으로 무화시켜버리는 힘을 지닌 것이다.

고명철, 「'고독/그리움'을 휘감는 '동감(同感)—사랑'의 글쓰기」,

『건너편 섬』, 자음과모음, 2014.

Lee Kyung-ja has been working with the narrative prospects offered by the concerns of radical feminism more than any other writer in the field of Korean literature, and yet she rejects the current "militant feminism", with its ambitions for the same social power now held by men, as a project which can never achieve any real satisfaction. Instead of "militant feminism", Lee dreams of feminists engaged in a bold and open love that is universal as well as maternal, able to take in all conflict, all exclusion and all hatred, with the power to restore such situations to peace through a burning away of their barriers and divisions.

이 소설(장편『사랑과 상처』—인용자)의 의의는 1990년대 주류적 페미니즘이 무대 저편으로 밀어냈던, 가진 것도 없고, 사회나 역사로부터 어떤 혜택도 받지 못한 '무지 렁이' 여성을 반가부장제의 증인으로 내세웠다는 점에 있다. 물론 그 이전에도 종종 현대사의 격랑을 헤쳐온 여성들의 삶이 형상화되긴 했지만, 그것은 철저히 남성 들 시각의 포로였을 뿐이다. 갖은 시련에도 불구하고 남편과 자식을 위해 헌신하는 현모양처의 '허상'이 수도 없이 재생산되지 않았던가 말이다. 그러나 이 '들펭이' 는 그런 허깨비 같은 현모양처가 아니라, 성실성과 속 물 근성, 가학증과 피학증, 겸손과 허영기 등을 두루 갖 춘 '살아 있는' 인간의 모습을 하고 있다.

고미숙, 「'덴동어미'와 '이갈리아의 딸'을 넘어서」,

《당대비평》, 1998년 4호.

모든 소외당하고 억압받는 사람들의 이야기가 그렇 듯 봉건적·가부장적 억압과 자본주의적 수탈의 늪 속 에서 어디 하소연할 곳도 없는 이 땅의 여성들의 참경 에 대한 인간 일반으로서의 동정과 분노가 누를 수 없 이 솟구치고 또 한편으로는 이러한 억압과 수탈의 충실

Go Myeong-cheol, "Writing with 'Compassion and Love' that Embrace 'Solitude and Yearning,'" *Island on the Other Side* (Seoul: Jaeum and Moeum, 2014)

The novel, *Love and Injury*, is significant because it takes a "rather repulsive" woman and makes her a champion of the opposition to patriarchal repression—one who had had nothing, who had received none of the benefits that are supposed to come with living in society and none of the advantages that are supposed to have been brought through history or progress, a woman shoved from the stage of feminism in the 1990's by the major currents which then dominated that very phenomenon. Of course, there had been many previous cases in which the lives of women had been elevated to similar heroic levels by a female character's endurance through the adversities of modern times, but those women had all been mere prisoners, confined within a masculine perspective. They had indeed suffered from lack and loss, and yet they remained a multitude of reproductions, all projecting the same delusory model, the "good wife and wise mother", devoted only to her hus-

한 대리자인 남성의 한 사람으로서 섬뜩함과 서늘함이 등골을 타고 흐르는 것을 느끼게 된다.

이는 이 작가가 아주 오랜 시간과 노력을 바로 자신의 문제이기도 한 이 여성 문제에 집중해 온 데서 오는 당연한 결과라고 할 수 있다. 이 작가는 빈틈없는 심리묘사와 적절한 분석력, 그리고 고통받는 여성 일반에 대한 애정과 그 고통을 가하는 가부장적 사회구조에 대한 '불타는 적개심'을 하나하나의 작품 안에 집요하게 짜넣어 조금만큼의 어정쩡한 입장의 유보나 어설픈 화해도 용납하지 않는 차돌멩이 같은 작품을 만들어낸다.

김명인, 「이경자의 연작소설집 『절반의 실패』」, 『희망의 문학』, 풀빛, 1990.

비공식적 역사, 주변성에 세심한 애정의 눈길을 보내면서 작가는 새로운 이야기를 써나간다. 그것은 변방의 목소리인 사투리로 쓰여진, 문학성이나 합리성과는 거리가 먼 것으로 치부되어온 수다와 푸념, 신세 한탄 등 여성 구술언어로 기술한 그녀들의 역사(herstory)이다. 그리고 이 새로운 여성서사는 쇠락해 가는 것들, 누추한 것들, 자연과의 공생(共生)의 서사로 그 지평을 넓혀

band and children. This "snail" here, on the contrary, is not of that kind at all as, no mere puppet, she is given the shape and the substance of a "living" human individual, comprised of robust combinations of such qualities as sincerity and pretense, sadism and masochism, and modesty and vanity.

Go Mi-suk, "Beyond 'Tendong Mom' and 'Igalia's Daughter'," *Dangdae Bipyeong 4* (Korea, 1998)

As an ordinary human individual, I react to these spectacles of ruin, these women of our own country who have in this swamp of capitalistic exploitation no place to which they can bring their complaints against the repressive forces of feudalism and patriarchy, just as I react to all stories of those who have been crushed or relegated to the margins—with an explosion of sympathy and outrage beyond my control; and as a man, a supportive representative of that oppression and that exploitation, I am frightened, and there is a chill that runs the entire length of my spine.

These effects are only natural, as the writer, Lee Kyung-ja, has for so long devoted her time and her efforts to the problems faced by women, and as

간다.

김양선, 「누추한 일상에서 건져 올린 공생의 서사」,

《실천문학》, 2000년 봄호.

　화제작 『절반의 실패』는 당시 한국사회의 여성 문제
를 테마별로 구체화함으로써 페미니즘적 문제의식을
본격적으로 한국문단에 등재시켰다. '고부갈등' '맞벌이
아내' '폭력' '남편의 외도' 등으로 분류된 단편들의 배치
를 보더라도 이 작품집은 소재적으로나 주제적으로나
'작정하고' 페미니즘을 전면에 내세운 것이었다. 여성
문제에 대한 이 본격적인 문제의식이 등장한 것이 1988
년이었다는 점도 의미심장하다. 여기에서 『절반의 실
패』의 역사적 의미란 이중적이다. 최소한의 정치적 자
유와 삶의 존엄을 획득하기 위한 민중적 각성이 최고조
에 이른 시기에 이 작품이 태어났다는 점, 그것은 한편
으로 페미니즘적 문제의식, 여성으로서의 차이와 그러
므로 더욱 간절한 인간으로서의 존엄에 대한 열망이 결
코 인간 전체의 자유와 평등의 문제와 무관하지 않다는
것을 의미하며, 또 한편으로는 이 '인간 전체의 자유와
평등'이 '전체'에 자연적으로 귀속되지만은 않는 세부의

these problems are the problems she must face, herself. There is in Lee's work a quality like stone, which distinguishes all of her pieces with a certain solidity, their compact psychological descriptions and competent analyses woven together well with a general warmth for these oppressed women and with a "burning animosity" towards the social order responsible for their pain and the patriarchy which continues to inflict it.

Kim Myeong-in , "Failure of the Half: Lee Kyung-ja's
Collection of Serialized Short Stories,"
Literature of Hope (Seoul: Pulbit, 1990)

Here, the author is working out a story that is new, giving us a warm and detailed view of a history that is never formal and of its surrounding features. The voice in which it is written is that of a pioneer, a writer on the frontier, telling the stories of women from an insider's perspective and in the dialects spoken by women, themselves—the friendly chatter, the reluctant grumble, the plaintive lament, for example, even though these modes might fail according to the standard criteria of literature or those of rational discourse. This is women's

차이들을 포함하지만 또한 간과하고 있다는 비판의식을 드러내는 것이기도 하다. 이 문제의식은 이중적이면서 또한 동시적이다. 남녀의 차별과 그것의 극복 문제는 곧 쉽사리 일반화되지 않는 차이에 대한 첨예한 인식을 필요로 하며 그러나 근본적으로 인간의 자유와 평등을 지향하지 않는 한 일면적이다. '여성해방'은 곧 '인간해방'이라는 페미니즘의 오래된 캐치프레이즈는 그런 의미에서 언제나 현재형의 과제이기도 하다.

서영인, 「남존여비의 역사적 연원과 심리적 심층」,

《동리목월》, 2012년 가을호.

history, it is narrative history, and it is a new history, expanding towards new horizons, such as the
co-operation between history and its objects, and
the inclusion of both nature itself and material that
might otherwise be dismissed as either shabby or
in decline.

Kim Yang-sun , "Narratives of Mutual Existence Picked Up
from Dingy Everyday Lives," *Silcheonmunhak*, Spring, 2000)

It was publication of the controversial *Half Failure*
that enabled the critical feminist mind to make its
thorough entrance into the Korean literary world,
and to establish a definite place for itself with
themes that rendered concrete the special concerns of women within Korean society. As the
pieces were arranged so that each story would
bear a particular theme—the conflict between
mother-in-law and daughter-in-law, the married
woman with a job, domestic violence, a husband's
infidelity and women living in poverty, for example—this collection raised feminism to a position of
real prominence through the deliberate choice of
themes, worked out in fiction either as subject or
as object. It is important that we notice the date at

which this mature manifestation of the critical feminist mind appeared, as 1988 was a crucial year. Considered in historical terms, *Half Failure* is significant in two ways. Born during a public awakening, when the desire for fundamental political freedom and the demands for recognition of human dignity had reached a climax, this work first declared that the critical feminist mind and the particular conditions of a woman's life, which provoke an especially intense yearning in women for a recognition of their human dignity, were not without relation to campaigns for freedom and equality for all of humanity, and then it went further, drawing critical attention to the general failure to acknowledge how particular points within this "freedom and equality for all of humanity" rendered these campaigns open to less than "all". This critical position itself has two simultaneous dimensions. First, it states that sexual discrimination and its eradication require acute attention to inequality, as these are not easily rendered simple, and at the same time it reminds us that if this freedom and this equality are not meant for all of humanity, the result will not be whole. In this sense, the familiar feminist phrase, "women's liberation" implies "human liberation" and therefore bears a challenge that is always present.

Seo Yeong-in, "Predominance of Men over Women: Its Historical Foundation and Psychological Depth," *Dongri Mogwol*, Sept, 2012)

이경자

1948년 강원도 양양에서 태어났다. 양양여자고등학교 3학년 시절 숙명여자대학교에서 주최한 전국여고생 단편문학상에 「멎어버린 행진」이 입상하였고, 서라벌예술대학교(현 중앙대학교) 문예창작학과에 입학하면서 본격적으로 문학수업에 정진하였다.

1973년《서울신문》 신춘문예에 단편 「확인」이 당선되면서 작가의 길을 걷는다. 작품 활동 초기에는 주로 단편을 발표한 바, 단편 「복수」「할미소에서 생긴 일」「벽」「퇴행」 등을 묶어 첫 소설집 『할미소에서 생긴 일』(1984)을 출간하였다.

그런데 첫 소설집을 발간하기 이전 이경자는 결혼 생활을 하면서 한국사회의 오랜 가부장제 남근중심주의 아래 힘든 여성의 삶을 다룬 장편소설 『배반의 성』(1982)을 발표하면서 한국소설사에서 페미니스트의 선구적 면모를 보인다. 그의 이러한 진취적 소설 세계는 여성의 관점으로 쓰인 여성문제 연작소설 『절반의 실패』(1988) 출간과 함께 한국방송공사(KBS, 1989)에서 미

Lee Kyung-ja

Lee Kyung-ja was born in 1948 in Yangyang, in the South Korean province of Gangwon-do. As a senior at Yangyang Girls' High School, Lee entered a short fiction contest held by Sookmyung Women's University with her story "The Parade, Arrested", which earned her a prize and set her on the path of serious literary work, which she took up through matriculation in the creative writing program at Seorabeol College of Art (now Chungang University).

Lee made her professional literary debut at the 1973 *Seoul Shinmun* Spring Literary Contest, whose prize for fiction went to Lee's story, "Verification". Most of what she then wrote in those early years of her career was short fiction, in stories such as "Revenge", "Incident at Halmiso", "A Wall" and "Regression", among others, which were published together in 1984 as the collection, *Incident at Halmiso*.

In 1982, even before the collection of the early stories, Lee distinguished herself as a pioneer and an important figure in the history of Korean litera-

니시리즈로 제작돼 공중파로 방영되면서 사회적으로 엄청난 파장을 일으켰다. 드라마의 성공과 베스트셀러의 반열에 들어선 『절반의 실패』는 한국사회의 해묵은 고부간의 갈등, 맞벌이 아내, 남편의 외도, 가정폭력, 매춘, 이혼, 빈민여성의 문제 등 가부장제의 억압적 현실에 직면한 다양한 여성문제를 정면으로 다뤘다. 이경자의 이러한 소설은 한국소설사에서 여성적 자의식을 래디컬하게 문제화한 것으로 페미니즘 소설의 대표작으로 평가받고 있다.

이러한 문제의식 아래 이후 소설집 『곱추네 사랑』(1990)을 발표하면서 한층 예각화한 여성적 자의식에 대한 사회적 반향을 일으키면서 '올해의 여성상'을 수상하였다. 그 후 이러한 그의 문제의식은 한국사회의 거대서사(해방공간, 한국전쟁, 휴전, 산업화시대) 속에서 좀 더 깊이 탐구된다. 장편소설 『사랑과 상처』(1999)는 그 대표작이다. 이 작품으로 그는 1999년 제4회 한무숙문학상을 수상하였다.

이경자의 여성적 소설쓰기는 장편소설 『그 매듭은 누가 풀까』(2001)를 계기로 여성성에 대한 근원을 탐구하게 되었고, 중국 운남성 소수민족의 모계사회를 경험하

ture with the publication of *The Castle of Betrayal*, a novel that takes a strong feminist approach to the difficult lives that married women have had to endure under the patriarchal systems of traditional Korean society.

The publication in 1988 of *Half Failure*, a series of stories noted for its focus on women's problems from a woman's point of view, made a tremendous impact on the Korean society of that time through the set's bold new ideas and innovative literary technique, and was adapted the very next year into a television series broadcast by the Korean Broadcasting System (K.B.S.). So popular was the book that one could almost say it had been a best-seller, and the television series enjoyed a clear success, so that *Half Failure* was quite effective as it raised questions about various perennial problems of women who face the repressive reality of the patriarchal systems of Korean society, such as the strife between mother-in-law and daughter-in-law, the infidelity of a husband, domestic violence, prostitution, divorce, poverty among women and the frequent opposition between the demands made by a woman's family and those made by her job. Esteemed as superior examples of feminist

면서 종래 그가 견지해 온 여성주의를 창조적으로 전복하고 넘어선 문명기행인 산문집『이경자, 모계사회를 찾다』(2001)를 발표한다. 이후 이경자의 소설 세계는 남성·여성의 대립적 시각에서 여성해방을 추구하는 게 아니라 이 모든 대립과 갈등을 근원적으로 치유하는 우주적 모성성에 대한 글쓰기로 나아간다. 따라서 이경자는 남성주의 사회가 이루어낸 경쟁과 소유의 극단적 문명에 환멸적 관심을 보이는 건 당연한 수순일지 모른다. 인류가 자연을 지배하기 이전의 시대에 신앙의 형태로 오랜 세월 치유와 위무를 담당했던 무속(巫俗)에 관심을 기울인 배경이 그러할 것이다. 장편『계화』는 한국 무속의 원형을 소설로서 복원하는 작업인데, 무(巫)의 여성 사제인 무당의 입문식, '내림굿'을 소재로 한 장편소설이다. 이경자가 쓴 장편『그 매듭은 누가 풀까』도 이러한 맥락에 닿아 있는 작품이다. 여성이 여성 정체성의 원형을 어떻게 훼손당하고 어떻게 굴절되며, 이것이 여성은 물론 남성에게도 어떤 병리적 삶을 살게 하는가에 대한 문학적 질문인 것이다.

최근 이경자의 소설 세계는 한층 심화·확장되고 있어, 한국전쟁과 분단의 현실 속에서 여성의 성장서사를

fiction for the radical ways in which they raise questions about female consciousness, the stories of Lee Kyung-ja have a solid place in the history of Korean fiction.

Exercising a heightened and more defined sense of the woman's identity, Lee dealt another blow to society in 1990 with *A Hunch-Back's Love,* a collection of stories in which she demonstrated an especially critical mind and for which she was recognized with that year's "Woman of the Year" award.

The same critical mind then turned to a profound investigation of the context created by the grand narrative of Korean society; among the primary subjects of this research, Lee studied the country's liberation from Japanese occupation, the Korean War, the cease-fire and the subsequent industrial era. The year 1999 saw the publication of the major work of that chapter in Lee's career: *Love and Injury,* for which Lee was awarded with the 4th Han Musuk Prize for Literature.

Still writing from a woman's perspective and speaking out in a feminist voice, Lee composed her novel of 2001, *Who Will Untie the Knot?*, as an inquiry into the very sources of femininity. She then spent time in the Chinese province of Yunnan,

다룬 장편『순이』(2010)를 발표함으로써 2012년 제1회 민중문학상의 본상을 수상하였고, 그간의 여성주의 작품 활동에 대한 평가로 2011년 제6회 고정희문학상을 수상했다. 그는 또 다른 장편『세 번째 집』(2013)에서 한국사회의 새로운 사회문제로 불거진 탈북자를 주인공으로 다룬다. 탈북문제의 뿌리가 일제식민지 시대의 강제 징집에 닿아 있으며 결국 태어난 곳으로부터 뿌리 뽑혀 당도한 새로운 사회에 적응이 불가능한 1세대 재일교포(일본), 2세대 귀국자(북조선), 3세대 탈북자(대한민국)의 난민적 삶에 역사적 궤를 깔았다. 이 소설은 우리 민족의 식민지 역사와 분단, 전쟁, 휴전에 이르는 과정을 탈북자 여성의 삶을 통해 드러냄으로서 분단극복 의지를 보여준 소설로 평가받는다. 이경자는 이 소설로 2014년 제19회 현대불교문학상과 2014년 제17회 한국가톨릭문학상을 동시 수상했다.

among a people of ethnic and racial minority whose traditional culture gave Lee an opportunity for direct contact with an actual matriarchal society, an experience that inspired her towards a creative move beyond the feminine identity to which she had clung in the past and informed her 2001 book of essays, *In Search of a Matriarchal Society With Lee Kyung-ja*. Lee's subsequent work turned away from the limited concerns of women's liberation in the conflict between male and female, as she set out towards a literature of universal maternity, in which there might reside more fundamental solutions to all such conflict and hostility. The interest Lee has taken in cultures of extreme competition and possession, established by men in accordance with masculine structures, may therefore be seen as a natural step towards an emancipation from illusion. And it seems to be in the same spirit that Lee has looked into shamanism, a religious practice which served humanity as medicine and as consolation for ages, until the subjugation of nature by human civilization came to pass. In her novel of 2005, *Gye-hwa*, whose focus is the ritual process of initiation whereby one becomes a shaman, Lee attempted to recover through fiction something of

Korean shamanism's original from. Indeed, *Who Will Untie the Knot?* had considered similar ideas. There, literature is used in order raise questions about how a woman's natural identity may be assaulted and distorted, and how such abuse pulls both men and women into lives of pathological neurosis.

In recent years, there have been yet more depth and an even greater scope in Lee's work, as in the novel, *Sun-ni*, for which Lee was recognized with the 1st People's Literary Award in 2010 and in which she examined how women's understanding of themselves evolved during the Korean War and how reality came to be fractured for women, while Lee also received the 6th Go Jeong-hee Prize for all she had accomplished for feminism throughout her career in 2011. For *The Third House*, the novel she published in 2013, Lee created a defector from North Korea, a main character who enabled Lee to address some of the prominent challenges with which such immigration was then presenting Korean society. The phenomenon of defection has its origins in the Japanese occupation of Korea, during which Korean men were drafted into military service and forced to leave their homes for Japan; a subsequent migration was made within the second generation, which brought many of the families back to the peninsula, but to the North; among the third generation, then, there have been many defectors to South Korea, where they remain detached from their ancestral homes and cannot adjust to the new society in which they have arrived—and so the lives of her fictional defectors allowed Lee to provide her story with a full historical context. Korea was indeed shattered by the historical conditions of the occupation, the political division, the war and the armistice; for its presentation of a will that, in the life of a woman who has come to this country as a defector, rises above the problems of separation, this novel has been lauded with critical praise. In fact, the book has brought Lee Kyung-ja both the 19th Buddhist Literary Award and 17th Catholic Literary Award in 2014.

번역 **장정화, 앤드류 제임스 키스트** Translated by Chang Chung-hwa (Chloe Keast) and Andrew James Keast

장정화는 2007년부터 한국의 현대 소설과 동화를 영어로 번역하는 일을 해왔다. 박성원의 소설 「캠핑카를 타고 울란바토르까지」를 공역하여 코리아타임즈 제44회 현대문학번역 장려상을 수상하였다. 박성원의 『도시는 무엇으로 이루어지는가』라는 단편소설집과 동화책 두 권은 한국문학번역원의 번역지원금을 받아 번역하였다. 2013년에 앤드류 제임스 키스트와 배수아의 「회색 時」를 공역하였고, 바이링궐 에디션 한국 대표 소설 시리즈에 수록되었다.

Chang Chung-hwa has been working on the translation of Korean literature since 2007, with a focus on modern fiction and children's stories. She received the Modern Korean Literature Translation Commendation Prize sponsored by *The Korea Times* in 2013 with Park Seong-won's "By Motor-Home to Ulan Bator." For three of her projects—the collection of short stories, *What Is It That Makes Up a City?* by Park Seong-won, and two books for young children—she has been supported by grants from the Literature Translation Institute of Korea. In 2013, Ms. Chang collaborated with Andrew Keast on an English translation of Bae Su-ah's "Time In Gray," which was published in this series of Bi-lingual Edition Modern Korean Fiction.

앤드류 제임스 키스트는 박성원의 소설 「캠핑카를 타고 울란바토르까지」를 공역하여 제44회 현대문학번역 장려상을 수상하였다. 장정화와 공역한 배수아의 「회색 時」는 그의 첫 작품으로 2013년에 출간되었다. 한국문학번역원에서 박성원의 단편집 『도시는 무엇으로 이루어지는가』와 동화책 두 권으로 한국문학번역원에서 번역 지원을 받았다. 이외에도 여러 작품의 번역에 참여했으며 앞으로도 더 많은 작품의 번역, 출판에 참여하면서 언어적 기술을 더 연마하고자 매진하고 있다.

Working with Chang Chung hwa, Andrew James Keast received the Modern Korean Literature Translation Commendation Prize in 2013 for an English translation of Park Seong-won's "By Motor-Home to Ulan Bator." His first published work, a translation of Bae Su-ah's "Time In Gray," also produced in collaboration with Chang Chung hwa, was released in 2013. Mr. Keast has also worked on a variety of other projects, and three of these have been supported by grants from the Literature Translation Institute of Korea—two books for children, and Park Seong-won's collection of short stories, *What Is It That Makes Up a City?* He looks forward to the completion of more work for publication—and always to the further cultivation of his linguistic skills.

감수 **전승희, 데이비드 윌리엄 홍**

Edited by Jeon Seung-hee and David William Hong

전승희는 서울대학교와 하버드대학교에서 영문학과 비교문학으로 박사 학위를 받았으며, 현재 하버드대학교 한국학 연구소의 연구원으로 재직하며 아시아 문예 계간지 《ASIA》 편집위원으로 활동 중이다. 현대 한국문학 및 세계문학을 다룬 논문을 다수 발표했으며, 바흐친의 『장편소설과 민중언어』, 제인 오스틴의 『오만과 편견』 등을 공역했다. 1988년 한국여성연구소의 창립과 《여성과 사회》의 창간에 참여했고, 2002년부터 보스턴 지역 피학대 여성을 위한 단체인 '트랜지션하우스' 운영에 참여해 왔다. 2006년 하버드대학교 한국학 연구소에서 '한국 현대사와 기억'을 주제로 한 워크숍을 주관했다.

Jeon Seung-hee is a member of the Editorial Board of *ASIA*, is a Fellow at the Korea Institute, Harvard University. She received a Ph.D. in English Literature from Seoul National University and a Ph.D. in Comparative Literature from Harvard University. She has presented and published numerous papers on modern Korean and world literature. She is also a co-translator of Mikhail Bakhtin's *Novel and the People's Culture* and Jane Austen's *Pride and Prejudice*. She is a founding member of the Korean Women's Studies Institute and of the biannual Women's Studies' journal *Women and Society* (1988), and she has been working at 'Transition House,' the first and oldest shelter for battered women in New England. She organized a workshop entitled "The Politics of Memory in Modern Korea" at the Korea Institute, Harvard University, in 2006. She also served as an advising committee member for the Asia-Africa Literature Festival in 2007 and for the POSCO Asian Literature Forum in 2008.

데이비드 윌리엄 홍은 미국 일리노이주 시카고에서 태어났다. 일리노이대학교에서 영문학을, 뉴욕대학교에서 영어교육을 공부했다. 지난 2년간 서울에 거주하면서 처음으로 한국인과 아시아계 미국인 문학에 깊이 몰두할 기회를 가졌다. 현재 뉴욕에서 거주하며 강의와 저술 활동을 한다.

David William Hong was born in 1986 in Chicago, Illinois. He studied English Literature at the University of Illinois and English Education at New York University. For the past two years, he lived in Seoul, South Korea, where he was able to immerse himself in Korean and Asian-American literature for the first time. Currently, he lives in New York City, teaching and writing.

바이링궐 에디션 한국 대표 소설 076
언니를 놓치다

2014년 11월 14일 초판 1쇄 발행

지은이 이경자 | **옮긴이** 장정화, 앤드류 제임스 키스트 | **펴낸이** 김재범
감수 전승희, 데이비드 윌리엄 홍 | **기획위원** 정은경, 전성태, 이경재
편집 정수인, 이은혜, 김형욱, 윤단비 | **관리** 박신영 | **디자인** 이춘희
펴낸곳 (주)아시아 | **출판등록** 2006년 1월 27일 제406-2006-000004호
주소 서울특별시 동작구 서달로 161-1(흑석동 100-16)
전화 02.821.5055 | **팩스** 02.821.5057 | **홈페이지** www.bookasia.org
ISBN 979-11-5662-049-5 (set) | 979-11-5662-050-1 (04810)
값은 뒤표지에 있습니다.

Bi-lingual Edition Modern Korean Literature 076
Losing a Sister

Written by Lee Kyung-ja | **Translated by** Chang Chung-hwa and Andrew James Keast
Published by Asia Publishers | 161-1, Seodal-ro, Dongjak-gu, Seoul, Korea
Homepage Address www.bookasia.org | **Tel**. (822).821.5055 | **Fax**. (822).821.5057
First published in Korea by Asia Publishers 2014
ISBN 979-11-5662-049-5 (set) | 979-11-5662-050-1 (04810)

바이링궐 에디션 한국 대표 소설

한국문학의 가장 중요하고 첨예한 문제의식을 가진 작가들의 대표작을 주제별로 선정!
하버드 한국학 연구원 및 세계 각국의 한국문학 전문 번역진이 참여한 번역 시리즈!
미국 하버드대학교와 컬럼비아대학교 동아시아학과, 캐나다 브리티시컬럼비아대학교 아시아
학과 등 해외 대학에서 교재로 채택!

바이링궐 에디션 한국 대표 소설 set 1

분단 Division

01 병신과 머저리-**이청준** The Wounded-**Yi Cheong-jun**
02 어둠의 혼-**김원일** Soul of Darkness-**Kim Won-il**
03 순이삼촌-**현기영** Sun-i Samch'on-**Hyun Ki-young**
04 엄마의 말뚝 1-**박완서** Mother's Stake I-**Park Wan-suh**
05 유형의 땅-**조정래** The Land of the Banished-**Jo Jung-rae**

산업화 Industrialization

06 무진기행-**김승옥** Record of a Journey to Mujin-**Kim Seung-ok**
07 삼포 가는 길-**황석영** The Road to Sampo-**Hwang Sok-yong**
08 아홉 켤레의 구두로 남은 사내-**윤흥길** The Man Who Was Left as Nine Pairs
of Shoes-**Yun Heung-gil**
09 돌아온 우리의 친구-**신상웅** Our Friend's Homecoming-**Shin Sang-ung**
10 원미동 시인-**양귀자** The Poet of Wŏnmi-dong-**Yang Kwi-ja**

여성 Women

11 중국인 거리-**오정희** Chinatown-**Oh Jung-hee**
12 풍금이 있던 자리-**신경숙** The Place Where the Harmonium Was-**Shin
Kyung-sook**
13 하나코는 없다-**최윤** The Last of Hanak'o-**Ch'oe Yun**
14 인간에 대한 예의-**공지영** Human Decency-**Gong Ji-young**
15 빈처-**은희경** Poor Man's Wife-**Eun Hee-kyung**

바이링궐 에디션 한국 대표 소설 set 2

자유 Liberty

16 필론의 돼지-**이문열** Pilon's Pig-**Yi Mun-yol**
17 슬로우 불릿-**이대환** Slow Bullet-**Lee Dae-hwan**
18 직선과 독가스-**임철우** Straight Lines and Poison Gas-**Lim Chul-woo**
19 깃발-**홍희담** The Flag-**Hong Hee-dam**
20 새벽 출정-**방현석** Off to Battle at Dawn-**Bang Hyeon-seok**

금기와 욕망 Taboo and Desire